Brightwater ATHENA

ELLEN BRADY FINN

All rights reserved. All characters appearing in this work are fictitious. Any resemblance to real persons, living or dead is purely coincidental.

No part of this publication may be reproduced, distributed, or transmitted in any form or by any means, including photocopying, recording, or other electronic or mechanical methods, either now known or unknown, without the written permission of the publisher, except in the case of brief quotations embodied in critical reviews and certain other noncommercial uses permitted by copyright law. For permission requests, write to the publisher, "Attention: Permissions Coordinator", at the address below.

Grey Wolfe Publishing, LLC
PO Box 1088
Birmingham, Michigan 48009
www.GreyWolfePublishing.com

© 2014 Ellen Brady Finn
Published by Grey Wolfe Publishing, LLC
www.GreyWolfePublishing.com
All Rights Reserved

ISBN: 978-1-62828-053-1
Library of Congress Control Number: 2014953991

The Brightwater Athena

Ellen Brady Finn

Dedication

To the memory of Tom, who enjoyed the story, and to our wonderful family: Tony; Mary; Louise; Alan; Lucy; Dean; Will; Cindy; Katy; Ross; Matt; Max; Angel; Anny; Emily; and Ellen.

Acknowledgements

I am grateful to Gerry Finn, and Upton and Sally Brady; who gave help and encouragement in the early stages of the book.

I also thank my friends in the Writers' Corner at the BASCC: Dee Trainor, Sara Burnside, Celia Ransom, Dora Saber, Sheila Becker, and, especially my editor Evelyn M. Zimmer and publisher Diana Kathryn Plopa, for their help and enthusiastic support.

CHAPTER ONE

It seems strange to me now that while I was growing up my father never mentioned the name Brightwater. But then many things were never mentioned there at Oakhill Academy in the faculty apartment where, throughout my childhood, he perched in his worn Morris chair like an aging hawk mysteriously deprived of flight. I never knew why he, a once famous archeologist, was now a Latin master at a Midwestern boarding school for 'backward boys' as he used to quote in his scathing manner. Yet I knew that the manuscript that he worked on in his free time was about a little statue called the Brightwater Athena and that I had been named for it.

I saw the words occasionally when I dusted his desk. I also saw photographs of the Athena, and sometimes I glimpsed fragile old documents in Greek — papyri, palimpsests, and crumbling parchment — which he kept in a locked metal box.

It was those moments, I think, that allowed me to live so quietly, so dutifully, in those cramped rooms that smelled of pipe smoke and the exhaust from the school kitchen; never, it seemed, out of earshot of his quavering, querulous call of "Athena?" Sometimes I had to clench my hands until my fingernails dented my palms before I could answer calmly. For if he seemed like a hawk grounded, literally by a broken heart, I was, in my own mind, a caged wild bird beating against the bars, although I went through my days like a quiet industrious wren.

It was the papers in the locked box that reminded me that my life had not always been this way. When I was six, my parents had spent a summer excavating a site in Greece. I remembered the village of Agios Titos, white stucco houses with red tile roofs, dreaming in the sun against the backdrop of Mount Dikte, birthplace of the god Zeus. I remembered the ruin, a rambling villa about thirty-four hundred years old, with wide stairs and many rooms. Unlike its sister in time, the ruin at Knossos, it had never been artificially restored, but lay under the Greek sun, hardly disturbed since the earthquake of the fourteenth century B.C. My father wore a pith helmet as he talked to the foreman, who wore Cretan dress of baggy trousers and black boots and a black lace head cloth against the island wind.

My mother directed the students as they cleaned and classified the day's finds. She was young, small and slim, with curly black hair. She had a pretty laugh, like the ringing of distant bells. My father laughed too, in those long ago sunlit days.

I remembered lunches in the shade of the grape arbor when the heat had stilled the cicadas and the song of the nightingale and I drowsed on the lap of the great archeologist William Courtney, while he and his sixteen year old nephew Montero, one of the students, talked with my parents of Middle Minoan Three and Cycladic figurines.

That was our last summer together as a family. That winter, my mother was killed in a traffic accident near our hometown of Birmingham, Michigan during a blizzard with whiteout conditions. To this day when I pass the Shrine of the Little Flower, I still think of her. Mother's little car was found crushed between a snow bank and a rented moving van. The driver of the truck was never found. My father had planned to accompany her to an Oakhill Academy sports meet, but he and I had stayed home with the flu. He never really recovered from the shock and grief of the tragedy.

My father and I moved to the rooms on Faculty Row at Oakhill, and as the years passed his health steadily declined until there seemed to be nothing young about him except his brilliant eyes and classroom voice. But if he sometimes seemed my jailer, he was also my mentor and liberator. Oakhill Academy was a boys' school to which I was barred admission; and the colorful, crowded public high school, where I happily escaped each morning, offered neither Greek nor Latin. Too proud and shy to give me open affection, my father patiently tutored me each evening, giving me access to that magical world of my sixth summer beside which the suburbs around Oakhill Academy faded away.

Thus it was that I had always wanted to be an archeologist, like my parents and the Courtney men, for although Monty was only sixteen, he was tall for his age and, to me, far into adulthood. In fact, it was my passion for the pictures and the stories from the ancient world that led to my second great love; for, inspired by the television coverage of the Olympics and remembering the frescoes of the bull leapers of Knossos, I began to train as a gymnast when I was about seven. Over the years, my small build allowed me to excel at the sport. When I was eighteen, my scholarship to the university, to my father's ill-concealed scorn, was athletic rather than academic.

By the time I was in graduate school, my competitive days were over; but I was able to pay my rent by coaching high school students. I was in New York during Christmas vacation to watch one of my students compete in a major meet when I was reminded once again of the little city of Brightwater.

It was my first visit to New York, and I had taken time to visit the Fender Gallery in Greenwich Village. Jared Fender, the famous collector and art dealer, had given his name to the antiquities wing of a major New England museum so I was surprised at the seediness of the gallery. The paint was peeling from the woodwork, and the large, chilly rooms were half empty. As my eyes became accustomed to the dim light, I saw a man standing by the pedestal of a little Cycladic goddess, silhouetted against the dusty window, and my heart gave a leap of recognition.

Twenty years had not changed William Courtney. He was tall and lean, with shoulders almost disproportionately broad. His dark hair was touched with grey, but it was still thick and sprang from a high forehead above prominent cheekbones and a jutting nose.

"Mr. Courtney?" As the man turned, I realized my stupidity. I had thought that I recognized the William Courtney of twenty years before, but he would now be in his sixties, at least. This man was not yet forty. His eyes, instead of the Aegean blue I remembered, were opaque, almost black. His complexion was swarthy, and his smile was not quick, but slow and tight, like a wince of pain.

In that moment, he seemed as startled as I, for he was before me in a stride, bending to lay his hand on my shoulder and scrutinize my face.

"No," he said. "Jared Fender. But you were hoping to meet Montero Courtney?"

"No. No, I don't know him. At all. I mean, except by reputation, of course. I'm sorry. But you reminded me of his uncle. William Courtney. As he was twenty years ago. I met him then." I felt a sudden anger at the grip on my shoulder, at the assumption of a familiarity that I did not share. I freed myself from his hand, but he continued to stare.

"And you are surely not Sophie Stephenakis of twenty years ago," he said.

"No. She was my mother."

"Of course. I remember. I'm sorry." He kept his dark gaze fixed on my face. "About your father, too. A car crash, wasn't it? Near Detroit? A terrible tragedy. A terrible loss to the art world."

"Oh no. My mother died in the crash when I was six, but my father is still alive, teaching at Oakhill Academy in Michigan." Such a start went through his body that I almost felt it myself, like an electric shock, although I had freed myself from his grip.

"Robert Grey? Alive?" He turned and walked away from me and stood at the window. For a minute his shoulders rose and fell as if he were short of breath. Beyond him I saw the street and the New York traffic and in the distance the arch of Washington Square, grey in the December afternoon.

The front door of the gallery opened, and he shrugged, shot his cuffs, and turned around, his long, dark face impassive. "Forgive me. This is very good news indeed." His height, which caused him to bend down to speak to me, gave him an air of concern, almost sympathy, although his eyes were unreadable. "You, of course, must be the daughter, Athena. I must speak to a client now, but may I see you again? Will you come to dinner with me?"

Dinner with Jared Fender -- that would be something to tell my fellow graduate students. "Thank you."

"May I pick you up at five? That would give us time to see something of the city. But you have been here before."

"No. Never."

The slow smile touched his face with its hint of pain. He bowed slightly. "Five o'clock, then. Where are you staying?"

"At the Hilton. With the U.S.G.F. teams."

"I will be downstairs. Between those dreadful sphinxes, at five. Until then."

He turned to speak to the new arrivals, a portly couple in yellow tartan from Burberry's. Although I would have liked to see his collection — I had saved up some money in hopes of bringing back a coin or other small treasure — I felt constrained now in his presence and let myself quietly out the door.

A fine, chill rain was falling, but I walked all the way up Fifth Avenue and across 52nd Street to the hotel. I was filled with a restless excitement, inspired partly by the city, with its crowds and its energy and its pre-Christmas finery, but mostly — I had to admit it to myself — by the prospect of seeing more of a man whose physical magnetism matched his professional reputation. I could still feel the warmth of his hand on my shoulder and the strange shock, like an electric current, that had passed from his body to mine.

Dressed for dinner, I frowned at my reflection in the mirror. I am small and thin with large dark eyes and short near-black curls. I wished I were tall and svelte. Even my best dress of Indian embroidery, perfectly suitable in Bohemian Ann Arbor, looked cheap and arty in New York.

My student's mother had accompanied us to the meet, so I called her on my cell phone. "Hi, Mrs. Smith. Athena Grey. I missed the floor exercises. How did Amy do?"

"You should have been there. She placed third."

"Awesome! I'm sorry I missed it. Tell her I am really proud. I can't join you for dinner. I am going out with a friend."

"A date?"

I felt myself blush. "Hardly. An old family friend. I'll see you tomorrow. Congratulations to Amy."

Stepping out of the elevator, I recognized him before he saw me. He wore a dark suit and foulard tie, but the elegance of his dress only accentuated something barbaric about his face, as if it were some ancient mask found in a primeval ruin.

"There you are, Athena," he took my coat from my arm and helped me into it, resting his hands for a moment on my shoulders, before we walked together into the crowds of Sixth Avenue.

"Evening, Mr. Fender," said the doorman. "Taxi, sir?"

"Have you seen the Metropolitan Museum?" Jared Fender asked as our taxi battled the traffic on our way uptown.

"Not yet."

"Come, then. We can at least see some antiquities before our dinner."

In the museum, standing before a Hellenistic victory, I finally asked, "How did you know my parents, Mr. Fender?"

"Jared. Please. Everyone in the business of ancient art knows of Robert and Sophie Grey and the Courtney expedition to the Agios Titos Minoan ruin. But I knew them years ago in Brightwater. I went to grade school with Montero Courtney, before I was sent to Cranbrook, near Detroit, for high school. They had an excellent art program."

"The Brightwater Athena is there. In Brightwater that is. Not Cranbrook. In the college museum, isn't it?" I said.

"Yes. The world's most exquisite fake. How do you know of the Brightwater Athena?"

"Oh, it's not a fake," I said, bending over a case of coins. His still bearing became even stiller. The long brown hand next to mine gripped the edge of the case.

"What makes you say that?" His voice was as expressionless as his face, yet I felt a chill. I stared up at him in silence. "Surely," he continued, "the expedition established without further doubt that it could not have come from that site. A Minoan villa from 1400 B.C. is hardly the place to find a long lost treasure from the fifth century workshop of Phidias. The working model for the Athena Polias.

The young Montero Courtney's article proving that point made his reputation. Although I have always thought that it was really William's work. Even our wonder boy could not have produced such research as an undergraduate!" His voice betrayed a contempt beyond schoolboy rivalry.

"Yes. Of course. How silly of me." His eyes held mine.

"There was no provenance, no record of its previous history. Surely such a monument, a model from the hand of Phidias himself, would not have gone unrecorded for more than two thousand years."

I thought of the crumbling palimpsests, the Alexandrian papyri and Byzantine parchments in my father's locked metal box. I turned away.

"If there were," he mused, "she would be worth — well, every museum and collector in the world would bid for her." There was a long silence as I moved along the exhibits, my back to him. I was aware that we were alone in the room. When he spoke again, his voice was so low that I could barely hear it. "Don't blame yourself for your indiscretion, my dear. I read minds. My grandmother was a gypsy clairvoyant."

Before I could respond to this extraordinary remark, he took my arm and led me out. In the taxi on the way to a nearby bistro, he began to tell me of the travels he had undertaken and the dangers he had undergone in seeking out his most famous finds. He did not confine his searches to works of art, but would obtain anything from the natural kingdom as well, as long as the collector or institution was willing to pay him.

"Next month — over there, by the way, is the Frick — I go to Brazil, where a retired empire builder wants to sell me a head by Skopas and a snake."

"A snake?"

"A bushmaster. The only one in captivity. A herpetologist has made me a tempting offer. Believe me, I am carrying it in a very strong cage."

"Your reputation seems to be richly deserved."

"May I take that as a compliment?"

"I should have said good reputation."

At the restaurant he was once again greeted by name. A waiter brought us a bottle of champagne in a silver bucket and placed before us two little bowls of caviar, each embedded in crushed ice. A couple in evening dress stopped to say, "Good evening, Mr. Fender." He bowed without speaking and filled my glass.

"How did you become an art dealer?" I asked.

"More or less by accident," he said. "I grew up in a big old house in Brightwater. It was full of beautiful things. My ancestors came in the seventeenth century, escaping the puritans and bringing their sculptures and paintings and furniture with them. My grandfather was a scholar who began teaching me about our treasures even before I was in school. And, of course, his wife, my grandmother, gave our family the gift of second sight, probably more useful in this business than knowledge."

I laughed, relaxing in the champagne aura. I wondered why I had found the fact so sinister half an hour earlier. *Overworked nerves*, I thought. *The chronic fatigue of the graduate student. Christmas vacation had come none too soon.*

"I sold a Jacobean sideboard to finance my first year at Harvard," he continued, "and discovered that I had a knack for it."

"So you didn't specialize in archeology at first?"

"Oh no. That was just a coincidence, a byproduct of my friendship with Montero and your father, who taught us both Latin and Greek at Brightwater Academy before I was sent off to boarding school at Cranbrook." He raised his glass. "And let us drink to the happy news of his good health. But tell me about the last twenty years. How have they been? And what are you doing now?"

The evening passed in light conversation, and it was not until we were parting at my hotel that Jared spoke seriously again, resting his hand once more on my shoulder. "You say that your father is working on the provenance of the Athena?"

"No. No. I don't know what his research is."

"Why did you say she wasn't a fake?"

"I must have been thinking of something else."

"You're a bad liar, Athena." His grip hurt my shoulder. I broke away and turned toward the elevator.

"Good night, Jared." When there was no response, I turned back, but he was walking away toward the revolving doors.

Although I dutifully spent Christmas Day at Oakhill with my father, I felt uneasy, even guilty, about my 'indiscretion', as Jared had called it, and did not mention this encounter to him. Instead, I listened politely to his scholarly diatribes, punctuated by silences only when he paused to re-light his pipe or lay a matchbook across the top as if to improve the draft, like holding a newspaper before the fire.

I was bored and impatient to resume my own life in Ann Arbor. He also seemed restless. When the telephone rang, he pounced on it, and his rare smile lit his face at the sound of a voice so resonant that I too, could hear it.

"I'm glad you called," my father said. "I think it's all set. Shall I take it to you there?" He glanced at me sideways. I refused to leave the room but pretended to read the Harvard Alumni Bulletin on the card table while I listened to the other voice.

"No," the caller said. "Save your strength. I called because I've booked a flight out from Boston. I'm at Logan now. I'll be there in a few hours. There have been some ... developments. Jared is suddenly back again for the first time in years and hovering around the Athena. Around Emma, too."

My father covered the receiver and looked over at me. His eyes were feverishly excited, but his face had the pinched, grey look I had seen too frequently in recent weeks. "Would you excuse us, Athena? Perhaps you could start dinner."

"Yes. Of course."

I went into the kitchen and, irritated at being dismissed, slammed all the drawers and cupboard doors. My father had a habit of leaving everything a little bit open. His kitchen always looked as if an earthquake had left each drawer and each door two inches away from where it should be. In his bedroom there were drawers which had not been closed for twenty years, from which handkerchiefs and socks depended, like laundry from the balconies of Rome. Usually this habit made me smile, but when I was annoyed at him I found it maddening.

I cut up onions and put them in butter in the iron frying pan. I strained my ears trying to overhear the telephone conversation, but my father kept his voice low. When he finally fell silent, I pushed open the swinging door from the kitchen to the living room.

Father was slumped in his chair holding his chest. "Get Bernie on the phone," he said, low. I dialed Bernie Brown, our doctor, who told me to call 911 at once. When I hung up the telephone, my father was sprawled across the card table, unconscious or dead. I couldn't tell.

CHAPTER TWO

Snatching the car keys from their hook, I noticed the key to my father's desk. With fumbling fingers I attached it to my own key ring. When I returned to the card table, he had turned his head sideways and opened his eyes.

"The papers. Where are they?" I demanded.

His face was grey and shining with sweat. "The box. The desk drawer."

"I'll lock them in the trunk of the car."

"Well done."

"Don't move. Stay here." I dashed out to the driveway, unlocked the trunk and threw in the box just as an ambulance, rescue truck and a fire engine drove up. The medics soon had my father on a gurney and loaded on to the ambulance.

"Will you ride with us or follow in your car?" the driver asked.

"I'll drive my car." I wanted to stay close to the papers.

"Don't forget to lock up." I ignored the advice, started my car, and followed the ambulance.

Bernie met us at the emergency room and took Father away on the gurney immediately. It was after midnight when he came down to the waiting room and told me that father had had a heart attack. "His heart's been bad for twenty years," he said. "I guess you knew that."

I shook my head, too appalled to speak.

"He had a couple of episodes last winter, but he didn't want you to know about them, afraid you'd quit school or something," Bernie went on. "His condition's stable now, and he's resting comfortably. You might as well go home, Athena. Get some sleep. I'll call you in the morning."

The lightly falling snow felt cool on my face as I stepped out into the night. It lay fresh and unmarked on the parking lot and the streets, but there were new tire marks on my driveway and footprints on the front walk. They dwarfed my own, and they led both toward and away from the front door. When I stepped into the living room, I felt at once the palpable aura of another presence.

"Anyone here?" I called.

The echo mocked me.

I looked at my grandmother's sideboard, which dominated one wall. Then I realized what was wrong. Every drawer was neatly closed. I went up the stairs and into my father's room and saw the same. I opened the top drawer of his bureau. His socks and handkerchiefs were folded in neat piles.

The very tall man of the footprints must have searched the house while I was at the hospital. I went back down to the living room and tried the drawer of his desk. It opened easily, for the lock had been chiseled free of the wood, leaving a white scar in the varnish. The drawer was empty of the clutter — mostly my father's *Homer* manuscript — under which he had habitually concealed the metal box.

I paced around the empty apartment, straining my ears in the silence of the night, too alert and watchful to consider sleep. Suddenly I heard the sound of a car engine in the deserted school grounds. I looked at the clock. It was two in the morning.

The car stopped before our entry. I heard the slam of the door and the crunch of footsteps in the snow. Hurriedly I turned off the lights and immediately regretted my action, which must have revealed that the apartment was inhabited. The doorbell rang. I crept into the front hall and stood on tiptoe to look through the peephole of the front door. Against the brightness of the snow-reflected street light, I saw the tall, broad-shouldered silhouette of a man I assumed to be Jared Fender.

I recoiled, looking around quickly. He knocked on the door.

There was a back door from the kitchen, but the path from there to the school quad had not been shoveled. My progress would be slow and my trail obvious. I heard a key in the lock. He must have found it in his searches. The door squeaked on its hinges. I shrank back into the hall closet. I did not breathe as he passed me. I heard his footsteps halt in the living room by the card table.

The telephone rang.

The voice that answered was not Jared's. It was deep and resonant, like the voice of an actor, the voice I had overheard hours before on my father's telephone. "Just a minute, please. Athena? Athena. Where are you?"

I came forward into the light. The man turned, and I stared in recognition. The resemblance to Jared was striking, but where Jared was all opaqueness, this man was all translucence and light. His complexion was fair, and his face was flushed with the cold. His large, deep set eyes were a dark sea blue and his dark hair was touched with grey.

"Montero Courtney?"

"Yes. But it's for you. Dr. Brown."

"Bernie?" My dry lips could hardly move.

"You'd better come back to the hospital, Athena. Your father has had another heart attack."

"Is he..."

"He's in intensive care. Who's with you?"

"An old student of my father."

"Good. Can you put him on the line?"

Montero Courtney took the receiver from me and spoke briefly before he hung it up. "I'll drive you there. Where's your coat?" He helped me into it and led me to his car, an airport rental parked behind ours. "Please God I'm not too late," were his only words on that tense drive.

Bernie met us at the hospital with the news that my father had survived the second attack and was responding to the medication but that his life was still in the balance. "You may go in and see him, Athena. He has asked for you." Bernie's lined face was grave and sympathetic.

My father looked very small among all the machines around him. I took his hand, and he raised mine to his lips. His eyes were huge and dark, with a look of regret, even apology.

"Montero Courtney is here," I said. A flicker of the old fire crossed his face. "Don't try to talk," I said. "You need your strength."

"But I must." The schoolmaster voice had faded to a wheeze. "I should have told you. The Athena. It's yours." I leaned closer.

"Where is it?" I asked.

"Courtney. Do what he says. Then you'll be free."

"Free?"

"From danger. Real danger. I never meant... Athena. Thanks. I only wanted you to be free. Now you will be."

"Nonsense," I whispered and took his hand. We had never been demonstrative, but he grasped my hand until the hawk's eyes once again closed. His grip slackened, and the nurse whispered that I could leave.

"We'll call you when he wakes up again."

Montero Courtney was standing by the window. He was wearing the corduroy trousers, moccasins and rumpled tweed jacket of the rustic professor that he was, but there was an archaic elegance in his bearing that made him seem an anachronism in this suburban hospital lounge. He looked like an eighteenth century gentleman from a world of open fires and polished tables and windows opening on to views of sailing vessels in peaceful harbors.

"How is he?"

"I think he's dying, Mr. Courtney."

"Monty. Please. Let's get you a cup of coffee."

He drew my hand over his arm, and the touch of his arm, warm and steady under the tweed, sent a transfusion of warmth through my body. The shock of physical attraction was so strong, especially at a time when I should have been feeling sorrow or at least numbness, that I inadvertently blurted, "But this is so weird."

"Weird?" He led me to a table in the cafeteria and soon returned with two cups of coffee. "Perhaps," he said, "or just natural."

Has he read my thoughts? I felt the color mounting to my face. I could think of nothing to say. A quick, singularly sweet smile lighted his eyes as I sat speechless. I concentrated on my coffee, which, strong and sweet, fortified and calmed me.

"You haven't changed much at all," he said at length. "You were always an old soul."

"Do you remember that summer in Agios Titos?" I asked.

"Remember? Of course." He was silent for a while, examining his cup as he rotated it in the saucer. "You used to say you wanted to be an archeologist. Do you still?"

"Oh yes. I passed my generals last spring. I'm a teaching fellow now in Ann Arbor, working on my dissertation."

"Well done." He said. "What will you do when you're finished?"

I thought of the saying among graduate students that the way to get a job in archeology is to shoot an existing archeologist. "I don't know. Ideally, of course, I would like to teach at a university and do field work. I know that money for excavations is scarce now, but still ... but there's also museum work."

"Would you consider a job in Brightwater, as my assistant, teaching and working in the museum?"

"Are you serious?"

"Of course. My current assistant isn't well. She will be retiring this spring."

"But ... if my father survives this ..."

"Robert loves Brightwater. He and Sophie would have come out long ago if she had lived. His heart trouble began when she died, you know. He should have retired long ago."

"I never knew. I guess there's a lot I never knew."

It had come to me over the past few hours how little I had understood the brilliant, remote man who had cared for me with such constancy all my life; and I realized that that constancy was in danger of being lost almost at the moment I had found it.

The abyss yawned and threatened to swallow me.

When Bernie, in his green scrubs, with a surgical mask at his throat like a macabre necklace, appeared in the doorway, the darkness almost claimed me. But I remained conscious, although there seemed to be no one inside me. A zombie walked with great poise to the old family doctor.

"I'm sorry, Athena. We did everything we could." The zombie accepted the half embrace of his kindly arm, was led to the hospital room where the sheeted white form seemed no emptier than I. I kissed the cool forehead and sat beside him, holding his hand. Bernie drew up the sheet.

"Is your friend still here? Good." Courtney's tall form rose over his shoulder. Bernie shook his hand. "Oakhill usually deals with the same undertaker. Does that suit you?"

I nodded, mute.

"Good, I'll have the desk call them right now."

"I'll be staying for a few days," Montero said to Bernie. Here's my cell phone number or you can leave any messages for me on the Greys' answering machine. I'll call the headmaster."

"Thanks. I'll be in touch." Bernie hurried away, silent in his hospital shoes.

Soon the undertaker arrived, a dignified, kindly man rolling a gurney. He shook our hands and agreed to meet us at the funeral home later in the day. He then nodded to Courtney, who led me away down some back stairs and out a side door into the hospital parking lot. The snow had resumed in the night and lay white and almost unmarked all the way to Woodward Avenue, where the early morning traffic was just beginning. It was still dark, but the eastern horizon had begun to grow pale with the dawn.

"A new day, Athena," he said. "A new life for you."

"Yes. Thank you," I said. As in a dream, I heard my father's words again and again. "Free. I wanted you to be free."

A seagull rose screaming from the edge of a garbage can and soared into the brightening sky as the lot began to fill with cars. *Free.* I felt a shudder, as if a new person were being shaken loose from the old dutiful Athena. *Free.*

"Are you okay?"

"I think so."

"I'll take you back to your house and stay as long as you need me."

Later, as he opened the car door for me in my driveway, I said, "You shouldn't ... I'm afraid I'm taking too much of your time." He took my hand to help me out and stood there for a minute, looking down at me, holding my hand in a firm grasp. He had good hands, dry and warm and hard, as if he did many things with them, washed dishes and tended gardens and comforted people who could feel no grief. I looked up, bewildered with the conflicting emotions beginning to penetrate my numbness. *Eyes had never been so blue.* I could have fallen into them.

"So. Now." His tone was brisk. "You'll need some sleep before people start calling." He kept my hand until we were inside the house. "Where's your room?"

"Upstairs."

"Go up and sleep. I'll be here if you need me." He raised my hand and covered it with his other one. "You've grown up beautiful, Athena. You used to have to hold on to my jeans because you couldn't reach my hand." We both began to laugh, but my laughter quickly turned to tears. He put his arms around me, and suddenly I was overwhelmed with weeping. He patiently held me until I was calm. His jacket was rough under my wet cheek, and I could feel his heartbeat, it was so strong. His hand became tangled in my hair. His cheek rested on my forehead, and when I finally collected myself and drew back, I saw that his eyes, too, were filled with tears.

"Thanks," I said, resorting to the old cliché as I regained my self-control. "I needed that."

"So did I," he said. "Now go and rest."

On legs like spaghetti I mounted the stairs, dropped my overcoat on the floor, lay down in my clothes, and slept until the telephone began to ring. I heard Montero answer it in the kitchen, so I washed my face and disciplined my hair. The apartment was filled with the light of the low, snow-reflected sun.

When I opened the front door to look for the newspaper, I saw the mark in the snow where the paper had landed. Leading to and from it were the same footprints that I had seen in the snow last night.

From the kitchen I heard the almost theatrical voice, deep and perfectly suited to a house of mourning. He was an actor indeed. He had searched my home, looking for my father's papers. Then he had acted the affectionate old friend and would continue to do so until he had what he came for, the locked box in my car trunk.

This handsome stranger who had momentarily seemed so attractive was nothing but a thieving hypocrite that my father had mistakenly trusted. My first reaction was anger, a flare-up of the fierce Greek temper I had long struggled to learn to subdue. If I had had the means to do him severe bodily harm at that moment, I would have. But as I stood in the snow glare calming down, I felt a curious sense of relief. I did not have to trust him. Two could play at this game. I had just escaped one form of domination only to be entrapped by another. I would bide my time but preserve my freedom.

The air sparkled. My eyes felt gritty. I turned back to the apartment and shut the door.

CHAPTER THREE

I walked carefully to the kitchen door where Montero was standing. He had just hung up the telephone. "That was Mr. Moody."

"The headmaster."

"Right." He pulled out a chair from the kitchen table. "Are you all right? You look so pale."

"Yes. No. I guess it's the shock, catching up with me."

"That's only natural." He pressed my shoulder, and I inadvertently flinched away. He drew back toward the sink, where he was silhouetted against the window. "I've made some coffee," he said. "After we've eaten I'll take you to the funeral home. Mr. Moody will meet us there. He has offered the school chapel and chaplain for the service— with your approval, of course."

"Thanks." I managed to drink some juice and coffee, but the cereal he put before me tasted like dust and ashes, so I soon pushed it aside. The doorbell rang, and he straightened up. "Shall I get it?"

"No thanks," I said, moving to the door.

It was Luis Gomez, slight and dark with lively eyes. He stretched out his arms to hug me, and for the first time in our long friendship I noticed how short he was. But his presence, as always, was a comfort.

"I came as soon as I heard," he said. "He was my best teacher. More like a father to me." Luis had come to Oakhill Academy very young, and as one of the foreign students too far from home to return except in summer, he had spent the shorter vacations playing with the faculty children across the echoing lawns of the school quadrangle. We had grown up together and had met again in a graduate linguistics course at the university. Like me, he was trying to finish his dissertation, and, after a year as a junior master at Oakhill, he had left for a more lucrative job as a Spanish teacher at the school where I coached gymnastics in Ann Arbor.

"Are you okay, Athena?" he asked, holding me at arms' length.

"Pretty okay. Thanks for coming."

"Let's go for a walk."

"The way we used to, Christmas vacation, when there was nobody around."

"I'll treat you to a Coke from the machine," he smiled. As he rummaged in the closet for my coat, I stepped back into the kitchen where Montero still leaned against the sink.

"I'm going for a walk," I said. "With an old friend. I'll be back soon."

"Of course. Take care."

Luis took my arm as we stepped out into the snow. "Who's the good looking guy in the kitchen?"

"An old friend of the family."

"Not the perfidious professor." Luis had been my confidant the previous year when my first love affair had ended abruptly when I discovered that the man I was hopelessly in love with had been married for fifteen years. Luis, too, had just had his heart broken when his childhood sweetheart had broken their engagement.

"God, no." We had reached the entrance to the student center, and I relinquished his arm.

"Sorry," he said. "Does it still hurt?"

"Does Maria still hurt?"

"Yeah. All the time." He fed coins into the pop machine and brought back two cans to the plastic table where we sat down.

"What is it that makes empty school rooms so dreary?" I finally burst out, to break the silence that had fallen between us

"My offer still holds," Luis said.

"Speaking of Maria and the perfidious professor?"

His eyes were somber. I put my hand over his. "Now I'm sorry," I said.

"You'll never get over him, will you?"

"Would you? At least Maria just found another guy. She hadn't been married all along, letting you make a complete fool of yourself ..."

"Fool enough at the time," he interrupted. "If I hadn't bumped into you that night, I'm not sure what I would have done."

"As it was, we both got pretty wasted," I smiled. "I haven't been able to look at a margarita since. Or even chips and salsa."

"And I ended up proposing. Are we still engaged?"

"I have thought of it more as an understanding," I said slowly. "We could count on each other unless something better came along. Or Maria was free. Is she?"

He looked down at his drink. "I don't know. I've heard rumors."

"Oh Luis. For your sake, I hope they're true."

"Do you? For your sake?"

"No," I said quietly. Betrayed in the innocent passion of first love, I had long since given up dreams of romance; but the steadiness of Luis's affection had been a bulwark for me all my life.

He picked up the two cans and lobbed them into the recycling bin and then stood up, extending his hand, and we began to walk back to Faculty Row. "So, Athena," he said at length, stopping by my door. "When I heard about Dr. Grey, I wanted to tell you that you can still count on me."

"Unless Maria comes back," I said with a smile.

"You know," Luis said, "my sister used to have this kind of sampler, embroidery, framed and hanging on the wall, one of her students had made it for her. It had all these little animals embroidered on it, and it said 'to love someone is to set them free.' I think about that sometimes."

"When the time comes," I said, "we'll know."

"But for now, still buddies?"

"Still buddies."

I raised my face, and we kissed lightly, in the way we always did, an old, familiar couple. He turned and walked away, and I let myself in the door. The telephone was ringing and Montero Courtney was answering it.

The next two days are a blur in my memory. Hundreds of people filed by to press my hand and murmur condolences. It seemed strange that such a solitary, retiring man should have so many mourners, but there were alumni from decades back as well as colleagues new and old and visiting archeologists still suntanned from the digs. Montero Courtney remained in the background, a quiet polite stranger, although he served as a pallbearer, opposite gigantic Mr. Feemster from the language department. I don't know where he slept, but he called for me each morning and brewed a pot of coffee, which we shared with polite small talk. As if aware of my withdrawal, he spoke little, but he was always nearby. He stayed beside me as the school chaplain committed the wooden coffin next to my mother's grave, and afterwards at the dreary lunch catered by the school cook. I had tried one forkful of mashed potatoes and mystery meat and pushed the rest around the plate.

When the last guest had departed and the class one boys were clearing the tables, we walked together to the rooms on Faculty Row. It was midafternoon of a raw day with a sky as dark grey as the dirty snow and slush, and my eyes and throat stung from the bitter air. When we reached the door, we turned to face each other. He was wearing a dark suit and sober tie, suitable for this melancholy occasion.

"Athena," he said.

"You have been very kind. I don't know what to say. I don't know how to thank you ..." I was interrupted by rapid footsteps behind me and a sepulchral voice speaking my name.

"Miss Grey. Please. Excuse me." I turned, recognizing the clothespole form of Edwin O'Neill esq., the school lawyer who had also done legal work for my father. He was an elderly bachelor and amateur classicist, and he had often added his anecdotal conversation and pawky humor to our small dinner table. He had been among the mourners pressing my hand, but his grey eyes, magnified by thick lenses, had filled up. He had withdrawn in embarrassment to the faculty room and missed our departure.

"Athena."

"Ned. This is Father's old friend, Montero Courtney."

"The archeologist. A pleasure, sir. Edwin O'Neill. Dr. Grey's, that is, Miss Grey's attorney." They shook hands. "Might I have a minute of your time, my dear? I'm afraid I need to talk business. Although, if you are unable at this time ..." his voice hovered delicately as if he hoped that I had my smelling salts.

"Yes, of course, Ned. Please come in."

"I'll come back later," Courtney said with a slight bow.

"No. Indeed and indeed no. You must stay. Strange as it seems, this concerns you as well."

"Sherry or tea, Ned?" I said as we took off our coats in the front hall, which smelled of the ghost of pipe smoke. "Or scotch?"

"Tea would be lovely on this raw day."

"I'll make it," Montero said. "You sit down, Athena." He had grown familiar with the kitchen. I sat on the edge of the Morris chair and Ned adjusted the sharp creases of his Brooks Brothers trousers and perched on the couch. We were silent until Montero emerged carrying a tray set with my grandmother's tea set and a plate of freshly made cinnamon toast.

"Oh my," said Mr. O'Neill as I poured out. He seemed to inhale a cup of tea and half of the toast before he wiped his buttery fingers on the linen napkin that Montero had somehow unearthed from the kitchen dresser. I grudgingly had to admire his thoroughness in searching a house. "That was lovely." He cleared his throat and his face, a professional deadpan dropping over it like a curtain. "You have probably guessed that I have come to see you about your dear father's, ah... will. He in fact was in my office last week to attach a codicil, and it is that which concerns you, Mr. Courtney. It is fortunate that you, ah... happened to appear on the scene, so to speak."

Oh for Christ's sake, get on with it, Ned. I poured a cup of tea for Montero, who was standing before the fireplace. His finger brushed mine, and they were icy cold. I tried some of my tea but couldn't swallow, so I put it aside.

"There has been an extraordinary discovery pertaining to the estate of your late mother, Sophia, the inheritance from her father Kostos Stephenakis." Montero shot me a look so intense it seemed to scorch my skin.

"Yes?" I said, struggling to keep all expression from my face and voice.

"It appears that some of your father's papers establish your ownership of a work of art. I have in my possession, entrusted to me by Robert Grey, an offer from a certain Bartholemew Badger, of Badger Steel, for ..." and he named a sum that made my head spin. "Upon receipt of this work, of course. You are perhaps familiar with the name of the Brightwater Athena?"

I felt the blood leave my face. Montero took a quick step toward me, but as I recovered myself, he returned to his stance by the fireplace, one elbow on the mantelpiece.

"Your father's will stipulates that you are to entrust to me the provenance of the Brightwater Athena until the will has been probated. Are you aware of the existence of such a box, Athena?"

I looked from one grave face to the other. Montero Courtney seemed to loom over me. I reached for my tea, but my hand was unsteady, so I put it back in my lap. "Yes," I said. After all, no hiding place could be safer than Ned's vault. "It's in the trunk of the car."

"Will you give it to me now?"

"Do I have a choice?"

"No."

"And then what?"

"After the will is probated, in a manner of a few months, your father instructs that we are to entrust the papers to Montero Courtney, who will be responsible for concluding the sale to Mr. Badger and ensuring that you receive your inheritance. Your father has named him your trustee." He drew the folded document from his brief case and handed it to me. I scanned it quickly and saw that it was all true. Mr. O'Neill cleared his throat again. "I am satisfied that your affairs will be in good hands, Athena. There may be difficulties, as you are doubtless aware, but Mr. Courtney is unusually well placed to deal with them."

"Difficulties?" I said.

"Concerning spurious claims of ownership by other parties." He placed his hands on his well-pressed knees and levered himself up in defiance of his rheumatism. "And now. If you would be so good as to open your car."

"Of course."

I led them outside and opened the trunk. Montero's hand reached for the box, but Ned prevented him. "In good time, my dear Courtney, I will be in touch with you."

It was only then that I noticed the police car at the curb. Mr. O'Neill shook Montero's hand, printed a kiss on my cheek, and loaded himself and my father's papers into the police car. We watched until it turned the corner and was out of sight.

CHAPTER FOUR

Once again we faced each other in the damp twilight. I extended my hand. "I guess this is good bye, then, at least for a time. I don't know how to thank you."

He took my hand in both of his. "You have no reason to trust me, Athena," he said. "You have scarcely met me."

Again he seemed to have read my mind. *Does he also have a Gypsy grandmother? Hmm, that would certainly explain the resemblance to Jared Fender.*

"But before I fly back to Boston tonight, would you have dinner with me? I have been making enquiries, and my fellow inmates at the motel tell me that I should dine in Greektown."

"I can't. I don't...I'm not hungry."

"Exactly. You haven't eaten enough for a mouse since I have been here. And I even made you some cinnamon toast."

I burst into a reluctant giggle. "You're supposed to be my trustee, not my guardian."

"But for now I'm all you've got."

"You are not," I blazed, jerking my hand free. "This is the twentieth century, Mr. Courtney. In case they haven't heard in Brightwater and whatever century they are in, women don't need guardians any more. I have been on my own since I earned my way through college — with a lot better scholarships than those old classics grant, in spite of Father's sneering. I am perfectly content with my freedom and independence. We happen to be thrown together by a legal technicality, but you are certainly not all I've got. In fact, I'd rather not think that I've got you at all. In any way."

His countenance did not appear to change so much as to freeze, becoming still and cold. He bowed slightly. "Very well, then," he said. "Until I hear from Mr. O'Neill. Good bye, Athena."

"Good bye, Montero."

As he turned and walked away, the campus street lights went on, catching a few snowflakes that swirled above his head. He walked slowly, one shoulder slightly raised. I thought suddenly of his steady, kindly presence through all the troubles of the past week and felt guilty for my outburst. *After all, what had he really done? Besides ransack my home... Trying to steal my treasure... which was now safe in a vault.*

I was still standing there when he reached the corner where his rented car was parked, and he turned under the street light, which emphasized the dark shadows of his eyes. I half raised my hand. He walked back and stood bending down. "Forgive me," he said. "I didn't mean to patronize you."

My temper, as always, had cooled as quickly as it had flared. "And I'm afraid I blamed you for my father's bossiness and then for his going and dying just when ... it wasn't you I was angry at."

The quick smile flashed, thawing his polite mask.

"You understand that I loved my father. But he could..."

"Yes. Robert did seem to have that effect on people." His expression changed to the predatory sharp-eyed look I knew so well, and in a perfect imitation of my father's schoolmaster voice, he intoned, "'Courtney, I know you are there. That ...hmm ... outburst will cost you five misdemeanor marks.' There. That's better. Have you forgiven me, Athena? Now come to dinner."

Before I could respond, he drew my arm through his and led me to his car, where he opened the passenger door for me and soon slid into the driver's side.

"Thank you. It was kind of you to ask," I said rather wryly, feeling once again that a decision had been made for me. "Monty! Watch out! For God's sake!" He had pulled out into the street without signaling or looking or even turning on his headlights, and a student roaring by in a corvette had nearly dusted him. The wail of his horn faded in the twilight.

"Sorry. I'm afraid I'm more at home in a sailboat than a car."

"Or a horse and buggy," I grumbled.

"Actually, yes. We still use them at Bluecove sometimes. Especially in winter."

"Bluecove?"

"My house. Now, how do I get to Greektown?"

I directed him straight down Woodward, afraid to expose us to the demands of the freeway. We did not speak on the drive into Detroit, he because he was concentrating on his driving and I

The Brightwater Athena   Ellen Brady Finn   ~ 37 ~

because of stark terror of that driving. When we parked in Greektown, I eased my grip on the edge of my seat.

Dmitri, the old waiter who had known me since I was a child, showed us to a table in the corner overlooking the street.

"Scotch or martini?" Montero asked me.

"Martini." There was no point demurring. Besides, I was aware that I needed it. When the drinks arrived, he raised his glass.

"To your bright future. Now what shall we order?"

"Saganaki is a Greektown tradition," I told him. When the melted cheese arrived and the flames were extinguished to the traditional "Opa!" from the surrounding booths, I realized how hungry I was. I spread cheese on the good Greek bread and devoured it. Montero signaled for another round of drinks.

"That's better," he said. I leaned back on the banquette, warm and relaxed and still hungry. The light of the little lantern on the table accentuated the hollows of his face, the cavernous luminous eyes, and the dark hair prematurely greying at the temples. On his right hand he wore a gold signet ring, so old that the device was almost worn away. His left hand was ring-less.

"You have been so kind," I said, "It seems to me so funny …" I broke off in a belated attempt at tact.

"That a man of thirty-six has never married?"

"That's the third time you've read my mind. Do you have a Gypsy grandmother too, like Jared Fender?"

The color left his face, and his eyes darkened. "Jared Fender? How do you know about him? Was he here?"

"I met him when I was in New York. I went to his gallery to buy something." His expression was still wary.

"He said he knew you," I said. "He looks something like you."

"Oh yes. My evil twin. We both grew up in Brightwater. Come from the two oldest families. All the old timers on Cape Brightwater— or the Point, as we call it— look alike, probably from intermarriages among the early settlers, when there was nobody else around."

"Why do you call him your evil twin?"

"Because I don't like him." He sounded every bit the New England Yankee he after all was. "Stay away from that one, Athena. He's no good." He turned to the waiter and ordered souvlakia and retsina.

"Yet he seemed very nice. Kind of sad, too."

"Yes. Very sad."

"But you haven't answered your own question," I pursued.

"Why has a man of thirty-six, with an international reputation as an archeologist never married?"

He studied the plate that the waiter put before him as if he could read an answer written there, "I haven't been free to marry. I have had ... responsibilities. I live with my mother and my Uncle William, who is retired from the University." The silence fell again.

"Do they need you?" I asked at length and again blamed myself for lack of tact. *Were they helpless, superannuated invalids,* I thought. *Or is that responsibility a woman rather than aged relations?*

The quick smile flashed ruefully. "Actually not. Will is a little lame from the collapse of a cyclopean wall at Agios Titos, but he drives everywhere. I took over the big house at Bluecove after my father died a few years ago, but I am sure that Mother would be delighted to move into the city. I have a little nephew who has been staying with us during my sister's difficult divorce and a son of my own, the result— I must be honest with you— of a youthful indiscretion."

My heart turned over. In spite of my nagging suspicion of him, I had felt a sense of proprietorship toward him from the moment he had loomed up in my father's house. I poked at the pilaf on the serving platter between us. It was cold and greasy. His long hand reached across the table and touched mine. I looked up.

"Are you going to finish that?" he asked. "If not, I will."

I forced my stiff features into a smile and pushed the platter across the table. "And you?" he said, attacking it with relish. "You must own every male heart in Ann Arbor."

"You flatter me."

"Well?"

"I have a good friend, but nothing serious. I was more or less burned by an unhappy relationship in college. A professor who turned out to be married."

"He hurt you, didn't he?"

"Yes."

"Give me his name and I'll straighten him out."

"Are you this overprotective with everyone?"

"Only you. And Willy and Victor, of course."

"Willy and Victor?"

"Willy's my nephew and Victor's my son."

"I don't like being overprotected, you know."

"I know," he said.

I concentrated on pushing the cold pilaf around my plate. The wine tasted of pine trees and the salt wind of Greece.

"Have you considered my offer of an assistantship in Brightwater?" he asked at length.

"I'm very grateful," I said, "but I have an obligation to the university until the end of April. Is there a chance that it would still be open until— say— the first of May?"

"That would be the outside, but ... yes ... early May would not be too late."

"Is there a deadline?"

He gave a sudden oddly humorless laugh. "There could be. Especially once the will is probated. He reached into an inside pocket, drew out a notebook and tore out a page. He wrote on it and handed it to me across the table. "Here are my address and telephone number and cellphone. The minute Mr. O'Neill gets in touch with you, call me right away. Do you understand?"

I nodded.

"Would you give me your Ann Arbor address and telephone number?" He handed me the notebook, and I wrote down the information.

"Do you have any living relatives?" he asked.

"Father mentioned a bachelor great uncle in Agios Titos."

"Michael Stephenakis. Yes. But otherwise you are alone in the world."

I nodded in silence. He leaned across the table.

"Athena. Come back to Brightwater with me. Tonight."

My heart seemed to swell as if it had been some shriveled dead thing suddenly exposed to sunshine and warmth and spring rain. "Oh, Monty. I wish I could. But you know I can't. There is so much ... and I start teaching again next week."

He dropped his gaze. "Yes. Of course. Forgive me. I can't help being concerned. There's a very real question of danger."

"You sound like my father."

"A wise man. Well. I'll be in touch with Mr. O'Neill, and as soon as you have the papers, I'll come back."

When I didn't answer, he motioned for the bill, paid the waiter, and stood up. "If you're finished then, we'd better go. My plane leaves at eleven."

"Thank you. That was good."

The return trip was as silent as the first, although for a different reason, since there was little traffic leaving the city. In the driveway he switched off the engine and said, "I really hate to leave you alone like this."

I was glad that the darkness hid my conflicting emotions. "I'll be okay. I have friends."

"Okay then. If you need anything, call me. Promise?"

"I promise."

"Especially if you should hear from Jared Fender."

"Jared?"

"Yes. Especially. Has he been out here?"

"Not that I know of." The suspicion that lay between us flared again. If it had not been so late, so close to his flight time, if I had not been so exhausted and still half stunned with grief, I would have asked if it had been he or Jared in the house that night. But I was afraid to disturb the fragile peace between us. I needed what little comfort he could give me.

"Well," he said, opening the door on his side. "I guess this is it." He helped me out my side and took my hand as we walked up the front path, slippery with slush. "Take care of yourself, Athena. Keep in touch."

Still neither of us moved. I looked up at his tall form looming over me in the dim light from the street lamp, which traced the hollow contour of his temple and cheek. "This is awful," I said at last. "I don't want to be an heiress or a millionaire. I just want my cantankerous old father back. I want to go in the house now and find him in the Morris chair demanding to know how my work is going."

"My dear." It was natural that as an old family friend he would bend and kiss my cheek and then put his arms around me, but then our embrace caught fire. He pressed me to him hard, for a long time.

We broke apart abruptly, aware of the neighbors, the streetlight, and the late hour. "Your airplane," I said. I was breathing hard.

"Damn my airplane. Athena. My dear. I'm sorry. I shouldn't have. Good bye."

"Good bye, Monty."

He strode away. I did not wait to see the car leave but let myself into the empty apartment. Once inside, I leaned my head against the cold wall and let the tears come. But they brought no relief to my heart. So after a minute I straightened my shoulders and dried my eyes, and turning on the light, began to pack my father's books in preparation for clearing his rooms for the next tenant.

CHAPTER FIVE

The winter weeks passed in a mind-numbing round of work as I taught Greek and Latin to university freshmen and tried to finish my thesis. I also coached a gymnastics team from a local high school to help pay my rent, and the girls did reasonably well. Indeed, they would have gone to the regional meet if they had not lost their last league competition on a rainy Sunday in March.

After the scores had been computed and the trophies awarded, the girls crowded around me, all except Brenda Bayne, who sulked on the bench. If she had competed, we would have won this meet; but she had lost her eligibility because of poor grades.

"Come on, Miss Grey. Time for the radochla," said the captain. It had started spontaneously the previous autumn, with the team demanding a bar routine from the coach before the equipment was put away. I was secretly proud that at the age of twenty-six I could still do it. I eyed the high bar for a minute. It seemed higher than it ever had before. I caught the low bar, cast back and reached for the high bar. But then a wrench in my shoulder sent me back to the mat.

The girls groaned in sympathy and gave a spattering of applause, but my heart was pounding as I rubbed my shoulder. The fear had been a little worse each time I had done the radochla throughout the winter, and I now knew that the fear had been justified. "Okay, kids," I said. "I'll see you tomorrow afternoon."

"And do the radochla then?"

"I'm like, yeah. Right." They giggled, dispersing toward the lockers, all except Brenda.

"We would have won. I could have skunked that girl on the beam. You wouldn't let me compete, so we lost."

"I couldn't, Brenda. You didn't have your eligibility."

"No other coach gives a shit about that. Dr. Batson says he's gonna talk to you."

"It's the league rule, Brenda," I said firmly, fishing in my gym bag for car keys and windbreaker. "Good night."

"You'll be hearing from Dr. Batson," Brenda said, "and my Dad."

The heavy artillery indeed, I mused, Bayne being the only jackass more pompous than Dr. Batson, the principal.

The evening was raw and damp, and as I drove home my headlights picked up filthy slush and passing cars crusted with mud and salt. The entry of my apartment house smelled of stale tobacco smoke, and my shoulder hurt like a toothache.

Flakes of rust and paint showered from my mailbox as I opened it. There was only one envelope inside. Dragging my bag with my good arm up the stairs, I took it to my apartment, where I opened it with fingers clumsy with cold. There was no letter inside, only a clipping from a newspaper:

> Brightwater. Immediate opening for graduate in Classical archeology. Curator and part time instructor in college museum in well-known seaside resort. Salary competitive. Call for appointment.

I laid it carefully on the dinette table next to my dirty breakfast plate and stack of ungraded tests, the detritus of another wasted week-end, and sank into the upholstered chair. It smelled of mold.

Who could have sent it? Why were they advertising when Montero Courtney has virtually promised me the job for the first of May? Be honest, my sterner self-admonished me. *You could have stayed in touch, but you didn't. After all he did for you. Whether you trust him or not, you didn't so much as write him a thank-you note. You deserve to be passed over, to be forgotten altogether.* But I knew that, discourteous though I might be, he would have kept his word.

I picked up the envelope again and noticed that it had been mailed from Royal Oak, a city close to Oakhill Academy, about forty miles from Ann Arbor. Of course. It must have been sent by Luis. In February I had sent him an advertisement for "Spanish tutor wanted to accompany girl student on Caribbean cruise." He could not have known how much the name Brightwater meant to me. I had thrown myself into so grueling a round of work that I was always too exhausted to dwell on the past and the memories of all that I had lost. But I was tired now. I leaned my head on the back of the chair, and after a while the clipping slipped from my fingers and I dreamt of Agios Titos.

The door buzzer startled me awake, cold and stiff. I had fallen asleep in my chair, and I suddenly felt as if my world had gone from color film to black and white. It buzzed again, although my watch said only seven in the morning. The peephole revealed the thinning shoulder-length hair, multiple earrings and studs, and beer bulge of my landlord. I opened the door.

"Ms. Grey, like, you know what today is?"

"March thirty-first. I told you I had to think about renewing the lease."

"Well ... like, you know?" Without changing his empty smile he shifted a toothpick from the center of his lower lip.

"What?"

"Like I gave you a break. You know, like your Dad being dead and all." In the silence that followed I could hear the traffic in the slush and darkness of the street outside. "We gotta meet expenses. Like the new rents gotta be fifty more dollars a month, okay?"

I opened my mouth but no word emerged.

"But like I said since I gave you a break, for this unit it's a hundred."

"A hundred dollars a month for a rent increase?"

"Take it or leave it, Ms. Grey. I got another tenant waiting."

"I'll let you know this evening," I said. I shut the door and fastened the chain lock. I scraped the garbage off yesterday's plate and spoke aloud. "A hundred dollars. I don't have it. I've got a multi-million dollar inheritance and I can't pay this bozo his rent." I turned on the radio, and the announcer seemed to reply.

"It is seven-ten and we have snow, sleet, and freezing rain. Traffic is stop and go on all major freeways." I snapped it off.

Half an hour later the telephone rang. "Ms. Grey? This is Dr. Batson's secretary. He wants to see you as soon as possible."

"I have a class at eleven," I said. "Could he see me in a few minutes?"

"He has no appointment at eight-thirty."

"Eight thirty then," I said and hung up.

Traffic on the way to the school skidded and crawled. The windshield wipers labored against the snow. "What shall I do? Where shall I live?" I asked, and the optimistic side of my mind answered, *you could always marry Luis. Why not?* Presumably the standing offer he had renewed before my father's funeral was still good. We still spent much of our free time together, going to cheap concerts and sharing meals. I was tired of this lonely struggle of an existence. I wanted a home. *We could make a home together, and I could grow to love him in time. After all, at twenty-six I was too old for dreams of romance.*

A new swirl of snow brought to mind the dark figure under the streetlight, the wild embrace in the driveway. *No romance indeed. Luis is safe. We would cash in my little statue and live happily, no, peacefully ever after,* I clutched the wheel, struggling to keep my car on the street and out of the ditch. My headlights picked up the dogcatcher's van in front of me and the barred back window against which the caged animals threw themselves again and again. Over the hiss of the sleet I could hear them yelping and crying.

In the parking lot of the school the wind peeled a McDonald's wrapper from the slush and slapped it against my ankle. To the right of the front door, the lights of the faculty room shone behind a row of bars intended for protection from soccer balls and other missiles. Within this cage the teachers drank coffee from politically correct non-Styrofoam and read the morning papers or worked on their grading. I paused for a moment out in the cold, feeling more isolated than usual from their easy companionship. The only one I knew was Luis. The others greeted me politely after gymnastics meets, but otherwise I was outside the world of their common labor.

I pulled my mind back from that pit of loneliness and self-pity and pulled open the school door. The corridor smelled of baloney sandwiches and sweat socks.

"And so I go 'Honest to God she hates me' and he goes, 'Don't worry I'll take care of it.' GOD. Like he goes, 'I'll have her job.' He was really mad. I mean totally." It was Brenda Bayne, and as I passed by, her voice changed to the immemorial chant with which students greet their teachers. "Good morning. Ms. Grey."

The laughter of the girls was punctuated by 'O. MY. God.' and 'I'm SURE' as I jostled my way to the faculty room. The bell rang for morning assembly. The home room teachers left. I poured a cup of coffee. Luiz was collecting his mail, and his teeth shone white with his radiant smile. "Athena, what brings you here so long before practice time?"

"Appointment with Dr. Batson."

"Well I'm glad you're here because I've got really good news."

"It's nice that somebody does."

"You just missed the great announcement," said the French teacher, raising her coffee cup as if it were a champagne glass.

"You know Maria," said Luiz.

"Of course I do. You've heard from her?"

"We had a long talk on Saturday. We're getting married in Mexico in June. I'm a lucky man."

"She's a lucky girl, Luis." Our embrace allowed me to compose my face over his shoulder. "That's great."

The bell rang for first hour. "What does Batsy want?" Luis asked, walking with me toward the office.

"I don't know, but I can guess. Brenda Bayne."

"And I'm the guy that flunked her. Some friend, huh?" I took his left hand briefly in my right.

"You've been a good friend, Luis,"

"Still buddies?"

"Always buddies. I'm very happy for you."

"So have a good one." He turned down the hall toward the language wing, and I noticed that there was a thin spot in the back of his hair. *He'll be bald before he's thirty*, thought.

As I waited in the principal's office — Dr. Batson made a point of keeping people waiting — I heard loud laughter from within. Mr. Bayne, portly, red-faced, head of the Boosters' cub, emerged and walked by without looking at me.

"Dr. Batson will see you now," said the secretary.

He was seated behind his enormous desk, a big man with a pendulous double chin. I sat down facing him.

"You asked to see me, Dr. Batson?"

He regarded me in silence for a long time, looking me up and down. He had taken a summer course in management communications and had affected long silences ever since. Finally, he was obliged to speak, "You seem to have a problem with the gymnastics team, Ms. Grey. Why did they not go to the regionals when they were at the top of their league?"

"I don't know."

"Isn't it a fact that you prevented the highest scorer from competing?"

"She had lost her eligibility, Mr. Batson."

"Dr. Batson."

"Dr. Batson."

"Didn't you get my memorandum?"

"Actually, I didn't." He swelled, as if not getting a memorandum were a personal insult. "Ms. Grey, we seem to have here a breakdown in communications."

"Eligibility for competition is a league rule, Dr. Batson. I can't change that."

"Are you aware of the penalty for subordination, Ms. Grey?"

Of course I was. It was written on the first page of my contract. I stood up. "Termination, Dr. Batson," I said. "But that won't be necessary because I am resigning first. I will send my resignation in writing to your secretary this morning." I turned and walked to the door.

He swelled again. "But there are two more league meets."

"Perhaps you and Mr. Bayne can coach them." With this Parthian shot I walked out and closed the door.

Boiling down the language wing to the outside door, I almost bumped into Luis as he was closing his classroom door. "Where are you going in such a hurry?" he asked.

"Maybe I'll follow your suggestion and go to Brightwater."

"Brightwater?" He was genuinely puzzled.

"You didn't send me the clipping?"

"Not I. What was the postmark?"

"Royal Oak." I put out my hand and shook his. "Good bye Luis. Good luck."

As I waved from the outside doorway, he was still standing outside his classroom, staring after me.

The sleet had ended, and daylight gleamed across the salted parking lot. A seagull rose and wheeled upward into the pewter sky. I watched its flight until it had disappeared in the distance toward the St. Lawrence Seaway and the open ocean.

The adrenaline rush which had sustained me through my moment of bravado had subsided however, by the time I crossed the "Diag", the university quad, toward my office. The loss of income, meager though it was, from my coaching job was not going to solve my rent problem. I still had no home. As picked up my mail, I greeted a fellow graduate student I knew only from meetings. "Hi, Bob. How are you on this dreary morning?"

"Well, good and bad. Libby and I want to get married, but she can't come here unless she can be a teaching fellow and there aren't any more jobs."

Marriage seems to be a late winter epidemic, I reflected. *I had almost caught it myself.* "What's her field?"

"Same as ours. Classical archeology."

"That's too bad."

Besides the usual junk mail, there was a personal letter in my box, addressed in a bold handwriting and stamped 'delayed by lack of zip code.' I took it into my cubicle and shut the door. The letter was written on paper with the Brightwater College Museum letterhead. The cursive writing had an eighteenth century character, as if it could have been written with a quill by a signer of the Declaration of Independence. It expressed pleasure at the chance to renew a friendship and regret that I might have seen the advertisement, published merely to fulfill a legal requirement. I was to be assured that the archeology department still awaited my response to their enquiry of January for the position of curator and teaching assistant, to be filled by the first of May. It was signed by Montero Courtney.

I leaned back in my chair, staring at the letter. It was so like him that it seemed to conjure his very presence. I was startled out of my daze by the ringing of the telephone. "Miss Grey? Edwin O'Neill here."

"Yes. Ned."

"Athena. Good news. The probate went perfectly, in spite of the obvious difficulties with the monument itself. But there is no need to trouble you with that, since Professor Courtney tells me that he has the situation well in hand."

"Difficulties?"

"Ah. Yes. Yes indeed. But none with the documents. None whatsoever. Your late father was clearly of sound mind, there are no contesting heirs, no relatives whatsoever, except for the uncle in Greece. The provenance is yours, my dear, and you are instructed to hand it over to Professor Courtney as soon as possible. I could undertake that errand myself." He sounded unenthusiastic.

"Actually, Ned," I interrupted. "I am on my way to Brightwater on business anyway. May I drop by your office today?"

"Drive carefully, Athena."

"I will, Ned. But don't worry. The salt trucks have been out."

Bob was still in the main office when I burst out of my cubicle. "Does Libby still need a job?" I asked.

"Yes." He looked bewildered.

"Come with me to the chairman. I've got to go east. There's a kind of emergency."

"Hey. Great."

It was not until I was on the highway from Ann Arbor to Ned's office near Oakhill that the full implications of my situation struck me. I was on my way to being a millionaire. I had never longed for fancy houses or cars or beautiful clothes, but archeology is an expensive business. Excavations have been abandoned, knowledge has been lost, because financing has been unavailable. Even the site at Agios Titos had been left half explored after that summer of twenty years ago because of lack of funds. I could be free forever of landlords and principals and students, free to travel, free to re-open the Courtney excavation and to regain the lost Eden of my childhood, the sun-radiant island where the nightingales sang. I had been so bound in by my cramped and narrow world that I had contemplated marriage to poor Luis. For the first time since my father died, I felt as if a great weight had been lifted from my heart.

Ned's office was a dark chamber in a mausoleum of a neo-classical building, and he unfolded his pin striped length and extended his hand to greet me, beaming. "Here we are at last." He twirled the dials on the gigantic safe, withdrew the metal box, and placed it in my hands with an air of ceremony. "I have written Professor Courtney. Let me know when you arrive in Brightwater, and of course, if there should be any legal difficulties ..."

"You'd be the first to know, Ned," I said, and he smiled. There was a moment's awkward silence before he extracted his watch from which a gold chain extended across his austere middle. He cleared his throat.

"Well, Ned. Thanks for everything," I said.

"I'll walk you to your car, Athena."

He escorted me out, helped me into my car as if I were an Edwardian belle, made sure that the papers were ensconced on the front seat. Then he spoke with great gravity. "It was your father's wish that, for your safety, the greatest possible secrecy be observed until the sale to Mr. Badger has been completed. You understand how serious this is, Athena."

"Yes, Ned. Thanks again. I'll be in touch." I leaned out the driver's window to kiss his cheek and then backed out into the street. He stood on the sidewalk, his brows drawn into a worried frown, until I had turned the corner and was out of sight.

Later, in my apartment, the telephone rang while I was filling cardboard cartons with my clothes and books. "Hello?"

"Miss Grey? This is Dr. Batson's secretary. He told me to make an appointment with you for a conference at 3:40."

"Well this is Miss Grey's secretary, and she has left town," I said and hung up, but not before I heard an explosive giggle at the other end of the line. Eat your heart out, Batsy. I stared at the telephone for a minute. Should I call Montero Courtney? I was seized by an odd combination of fear and longing. I didn't want to talk to him on the telephone. I wanted to be with him. *Be honest,* I thought. *He fascinates me. I want to know what he's up to. And I can't find out until he has the papers.* And there was something in his story, some discrepancy which I couldn't quite recall but which filled me with misgiving. *What was it?* In any case, there was nothing to prevent me from simply driving to Brightwater and then I would give him my father's papers.

Loading my clothes and books and the metal box into the car was easy, because the years of gymnastics have left me with unusual upper body strength. The apartment had been rented furnished, if the ugly appointments could be so described, and my father's few ancestral pieces were in storage with a moving company in Detroit.

I dashed off my letter of resignation to Batsy and left it in the outgoing mail. Then I locked my apartment door and left the key in the landlord's box. The salt trucks had been by again. The road opened before me, white and bare.

Only an occasional snowflake swirled by as I drove south to the freeway and through Detroit to the Ambassador Bridge to Canada. I stopped at Canadian Customs at the border on the other side of the river.

"Citizen of what country?"

"The United States."

"Anything to declare?"

Yes, I thought. *I want to declare that I have gone mad and quit two perfectly good jobs to go halfway across the country with a priceless set of documents to a place I have never seen.*

"No. Nothing." I nodded toward the backseat. "I am moving to New England by way of Buffalo, and I am taking my stuff with me."

"Drive over here."

All Detroiters, especially those under thirty, know "the Tank", the car park where the customs men search the car for marijuana or other contraband. I thought wistfully of the several times that, chaperoning student tours through Europe, I had simply bypassed customs through the previous arrangement of the couriers. Those summer jaunts through Italy and Greece seemed far away on this winter day in Canada.

The man came to the driver's window. He was holding the locked box. I opened the car door and stepped out into the snow. I had the curious sensation that my entire body had grown as cold and still as the landscape around me. My heart seemed not to beat. Without thinking I reached out to take the box. I had not opened it since the night my father died. Suddenly I had to know whether it was empty or full. He jerked it back slightly, the gesture of a teasing schoolboy; but his manner was dead serious.

"Come into the office, Miss."

I followed him into the building. "Open this please."

"Yes." I produced the little key from my chain, fitted it into the little lock, and raised the lid. The papers lay there safe, ancient, unchanged from the last time I had seen them, except for the topmost document which I saw at a glance was modern. The letterhead was from the Vatican Library, and the letter was written in Latin, dated the Ides of the previous December. It must have been the final link in my father's long chain of research, the cause of Montero's arrival at Oakhill.

My heart seemed to resume its beating, so loud that I was afraid the customs man would hear it. "It's manuscripts, research that I inherited from my late father," I said. "He was a teacher of Greek and Latin."

Wherever the British flag has flown, the words are magic. I thought of Gladstone's definition of a gentleman.

"Really old, eh?" said the customs man. "I remember my Latin teacher, a holy terror. He could have read these. Well. Any alcoholic beverages, firearms, or citrus fruits?"

"None."

"Thanks for your trouble then. Have a good trip, eh?"

"I will."

Outside of Buffalo I drove into a clearing of blue sky and snow dazzle, but bad weather overtook me again on the

Massachusetts Turnpike in the early hours of morning, so I spent the rest of the night in a cheap motel by the highway. The next morning, when I took the exit to Brightwater I nearly skidded into the ditch. It took me two hours in second gear to travel the next fifty miles, and when I finally stopped at a gas station at the top of a hill, I could scarcely uncurl my hands from the steering wheel.

From my parking place I could see the ocean, dark grey and streaked with foam against the snowy land, and the Brightwater Peninsula. It is joined to the continent by an isthmus divided by a canal so that it is a man-made island. The maps call it Cape Brightwater, but the natives call it Brightwater Point, or just the Point. The highway descended steeply past the ugly industrial city of New Stoke and then rose up a hill which blocked the view to the left but revealed the cable suspension Brightwater Bridge. A semitrailer had not made the first slope of the bridge but lay overturned across all four lanes of traffic. Twin snakes of cars wound along the hill on one side of the wreck and the bridge on the other.

I went inside the gas station to where the proprietor was talking to a bald old man with a weather beaten face, red-brown and deeply seamed.

"Excuse me," I said. "Is there any other way to get to Brightwater besides the interstate?"

"The soopahighway?" said the old man.

"Yes. There's a truck blocking it."

He considered me for a long time. "You going to the Point?"

"Yes."

He looked out through the dirty plate glass window. "That your little car?" I nodded.

"You got folks on the Point?" I was beginning to wonder if it were necessary to pass an oral exam to be allowed into Brightwater. The old man had blue blue eyes, creased in the corners as if from years of squinting against the sea glare. He wore a uniform like that of a policemen, except that it was devoid of insignia.

"No. I'm going there to look for a job."

"Not many jobs in Brightwater."

"I read an ad for a curator at the museum, and I'm qualified for it."

He gave a little start, as if from the spark that flashed and faded in his eyes. "How old are you?"

This was almost too much, but a compulsion to trust him caused me to answer, "Twenty-six."

"You don't look older than fourteen," he said.

"So I've been told." I smiled.

He seemed to ponder his words carefully before he spoke again. "You could take the Fenderbog Road."

Behind him, the young proprietor shifted uneasily. "You sending her out the Fenderbog Road alone, Gus?"

"That's a good little car," he responded. To me he added, "Lock your doors and keep the windows up."

"Even in summer," the proprietor said, "you always keep your windows up when you drive on the Fenderbog Road."

I looked back at the old man, who nodded.

"Very peculiar people," he said, "live on the Fenderbog Road."

He led me to the door and pointed to the turn-off, almost invisible in a stand of sumac and scrub oak. "Just follow the road to the old Turnpike Bridge. It's been condemned, but it's safe in this wind and tide. It's slack tide. Turn right after the bridge and it'll take you back to the main road. "You'll be all right," he said, "and you'll get good traction."

CHAPTER SIX

He was right about the traction, I thought as the scrub growth closed in behind me. The road had not been resurfaced in so long that it was virtually unpaved, and my Chevy Spark bounced and shook from one pothole to the next. I turned on the radio, but nothing could be heard except static. The first house I passed was a roofed-over basement with four ancient Cadillacs in the driveway. A skeleton of a dog, all ribs and fangs, burst from an overgrown hedge and chased me away, barking savagely. Next, a Victorian mansion stood empty with broken windowpanes and sagging porches, although lights shone cozily from a tarpaper lean-to along one side. Around a corner, I had to brake suddenly for a horse, which ambled across the road, stopping to probe the pavement for the dry grass growing up through the cracks. The bumps in the road formed a rhythmic accompaniment to my thoughts, like the drumbeats of a rock song. "You always keep your windows up— When you drive on the Fenderbog Road— Very peculiar people— Live on the Fenderbog Road."

My hands were cold, but the steering wheel was wet with sweat. I saw no other vehicle, going in either direction. The wind slatted frozen rain against the windshield in bursts. When I saw the low bridge, I sighed with relief, in spite of the red flag on its superstructure and the sign which read:

CAUTION
BRIDGE UNSAFE
PROCEED AT YOUR OWN RISK

The water of Brightwater Harbor rushed between the piers of the bridge, almost black, patched with whitecaps, into the canal. On the other side the land was fairly level, snowy fields bordered by stone walls. I passed a stone and iron gate which led to a long drive rising to a hilltop crowned with a large white eighteenth century wooden manor house spreading among wings and porticoes. A few miles beyond that, a blinking traffic light seemed to signal the end of the Fenderbog Road, for I soon saw a sign directing me to the exit back to the interstate.

Brightwater was a pretty little city, even on this forbidding morning. Old painted wooden houses faced each other across narrow cobbled streets and flagstone sidewalks. In the middle of town, the Episcopal Church raised its steeple from a graveyard at the end of a common set about with maple trees. I turned left up the slope of the hill where the university crowned the city. There was a collegiate gothic quadrangle, a replica of a fourteenth century college, similar to the law quad back in Ann Arbor, but the street in front of it was blocked by a tree limb blown down in the storm. A uniformed policeman was directing traffic away from it. When I stopped, he came to the door of the car, and I opened the window on my side.

"Excuse me, officer."

"Chief Porter. Ben Porter." He had a flat matter-of-fact voice like the detective on 'Dragnet.' "What can I do for you, Miss?"

"I'm looking for the Brightwater University Museum."

"Trapper's Castle?"

"Trapper's Castle?" I repeated stupidly. He took off his blue cap and scratched his thinning, sandy hair. He was compact and strongly built with light blue eyes in a suntanned face.

"It used to be the mansion of a man named Alfred Trapper, who donated it to the college, so here in Brightwater we've always called it Trapper's Castle. It's right down the hill here. If you back out here you can go straight down to Market Street, your last chance to turn left before the harbor, then take the first right across the causeway."

"Thank you, Chief Porter." I shifted into reverse.

"Hold it," he said. "I'll get you out of here." He stopped traffic in both directions until I was on my way with a grateful wave.

Alfred Trapper had built his monstrosity on an islet in Brightwater Harbor and connected it to the city by a one-lane walled causeway entered through a wrought iron and stone gateway. The effect was somewhere between Disneyland and a horror movie. *The security must make it easy to protect the art collection,* I thought.

The rain had stopped, but the wind had risen. I felt as if my car would be buffeted onto the sidewalk of the narrow street. The causeway was also narrow, and I slowed to a crawl to be sure not to scrape a side against one of the stone gateposts. The gates stood open, tall black iron bars, pointed at the top. With a chill, I thought of the dogcatcher's van in Ann Arbor.

The walls of the causeway were about four feet high, topped with broken glass and claustrophobically close, so it was a relief to emerge into the parking lot beneath the towers and battlements of Trapper's Castle, their stones indescribably bleak against the dark sea and sky. I clung to the balustrade to keep from being blown off the steps as I mounted to the forbidding portal.

The door opened on oiled hinges and admitted me to a great hall floored with flagstones covered with antique Persian rugs. Ahead of me twin staircases swept up to a gallery that ran the width of the hall. To my right, logs the size of small trees blazed in a fireplace. I had been cold and damp for so long that I went directly to the fender.

"May I help you?"

I had not noticed the desk next to the fire until a tall woman arose from behind it and glided toward me on a wave of Chanel Number Five. Her blonde hair was swept back from a face of classical perfection into a heavy chignon and her dress of auburn cashmere fell in graceful folds over her ample curves. Aware of the baggy sweater and pants that I had slept in, my boots streaked with salty slush, my hair whipped into a tangle by the wind, I felt the color rise to my face.

"I've come to apply for a job. As curator. I saw your advertisement ..."

"Oh, I'm sorry, Miss, but the job has already been taken."

I stood speechless. I had been so convinced that my destiny lay in Brightwater that the thought of rejection had not occurred to me. *Had I not been named for the Athena? Had I not come to claim her as my rightful inheritance?* "But I am qualified," I finally blurted out. "I have been offered the job."

She sighed and turned back to the desk, where she pressed a button and picked up the receiver. "Monty darling, there's a young girl here about the job you offered that woman in Michigan." Relief caused my knees to buckle, and I leaned against the desk.

He appeared at the top of the stairs. I noticed as if for the first time his height and the elegance of his bearing. If he had worn spurred boots and a saber and lace at his throat instead of rumpled tweeds' I would scarcely have noticed. He descended quickly. His sweet smile flashed and he bowed slightly over my hand. "Athena. You should have called or written. Did you get my letter?"

"Yes. Just yesterday. It was delayed because of not having a zip code."

"My fault entirely. It's hard enough to remember what Midwestern state has what initials, never mind the numbers. Emma, this is indeed Athena Grey, our candidate. Athena, this is Emma Trapper, our director of publicity." I started to extend my hand but quickly drew it back, chilled by Emma's frozen stance. She turned her head, but not before I had caught a look of such intense fear that I almost looked over my shoulder to see what might have inspired such horror.

"How do you do?" I said into the awkward silence. "Are you related to Alfred Trapper?"

She finally moved her hand and touched her chignon. "He was my grandfather," she said.

Guessing that I was calculating her age, she added, "He married my grandmother late in life. I am now the entire Trapper family. The last remaining heir. Are you ready for lunch, Monty, darling?"

"Would you mind waiting just a minute so that I can show Athena her desk and call Gus?" He turned to me. "Our custodian, but he belongs here more than anyone. His ancestors settled this island and gave it their name, Howe's island."

"And could I see the Athena?" I asked.

"Of course." His eyes were so warm that, standing between him and Emma, I felt as if I had the sun on my face and the cold wind on my back.

He led me up the stairs to the middle of the gallery, from which a vista opened up the length of the room, which had originally been the ballroom of Alfred Trapper's Castle. There were statues and display cases down both sides, but I had eyes only for the small figure in the glass case at the end of the room.

Barely eighteen inches high, the statue was executed with such majesty of conception and perfection of detail that it dwarfed everything else in the gallery. The youthful features in the ancient ivory face made her seem both young and old. Grave and serene, she wore a gold helmet and a chiton also of gold. Her left hand rested on a shield engraved in as much detail as that of Achilles, and in her right hand she held a tiny Victory. At her small feet was coiled the sacred snake Erichthonius.

A brass plate on the pedestal beneath her case read, "The Brightwater Athena. A chryselephantine replica, 19th century, of a fifth century B.C. work of Phidias. On Loan from the estate of Alfred Trapper."

The words seemed to explode in my brain. The estate of Alfred Trapper. Emma. The last remaining heir. Ned O'Neill's other party. I stood as motionless as the figure for whom I had been named. I was hers. She was mine. Not Emma's.

After a time I heard Montero Courtney's voice as if from a distance. "Your father's papers."

I spun around, my initial shock giving way to such anger that I could almost hear it roar and crackle like an inner blaze. We were alone in the gallery. "Do you have them?" The great eyes seemed to penetrate my brain.

I breathed deeply, forcing myself to think. I had earlier determined to give them to him as soon as I could see him alone, remembering both my father's and Ned's insistence on the importance of secrecy; but now I realized that I needed more time to understand my new situation and its many baffling elements — Emma's claim to ownership, her terror of me, the easy intimacy between her and Montero, the role of Jared Fender in all this mystery. I stared back at him, speechless.

At length he turned and strode ahead of me back to the hall. I had to hurry to catch up with him. "The key to the Athena's case has been missing for several weeks. If your predecessor Helen Adams knows where it is, she won't tell us. She is a very determined lady."

"Is she retired?" I asked.

"She was just about to retire. She had moved out of her suite here at the Castle and started interviewing applicants, but then I went out to see Robert, and while I was gone, she had some kind of attack and had to go to the hospital. She was out for a while but then had to go back again last week. I'll take you to meet her this afternoon. Perhaps she'll tell you where the key is. You seem so innocent and trustworthy."

Is he being sarcastic? His courteous manner made it impossible to tell.

"Now, I have promised to take Emma to lunch," he continued. "Miss Adams lived here in a suite of rooms in one of the castle towers before she retired. They are at your disposal if you would like them. There's no rent. It comes with the job. Would you like Mr. Howe to show them to you?"

"Oh yes. Please."

"Good." He flipped open his cell phone and spoke a few words and closed it again. "I'll arrange an appointment with Miss Adams at the hospital this afternoon, if she is up to it."

"I can't thank you..."

"You could," he began, but the throaty voice behind him interrupted.

"Monty darling."

"Yes, Emmy. Athena, this is Gus Howe. He helped Emma into a camel's hair coat. "Gus, this is Athena Grey, Robert and Sophie's daughter. She is taking Miss Adams' place."

I turned to meet the museum guard and recognized the old man who had sent me down the Fenderbog Road. "Need a hand with your luggage?" he said with a smile as he shook my hand.

I heard Emma's low laugh as the door closed behind her and Montero. Then I heard a car start up and roar across the causeway. "The way Monty speeds off this island," said Gus, "he's going to hurt himself someday."

"I got the job," I said, smiling.

"Eh yuh. Thought you would."

"You must have just about followed me here."

"Well. I don't hold with newcomers having to drive alone down the Fenderbog Road. But I stayed enough behind so's you wouldn't feel you were being followed."

"Thanks. That was good of you."

Out in the parking lot he loaded my suitcases and cartons of books onto a handcart while I carried the box of papers. An elevator clanked and swayed, carrying us to the third floor, where Gus held the door open for me. The passage took us past several spacious bedrooms furnished with massive antiques.

"They use these sometimes for putting up important guests, or they rent them out for meetings and conferences," said Gus. "And here's your place."

My new rooms were in one of the towers that fortified each corner of the castle. There was a sitting room with a semicircular wall, with windows and window seats commanding a view of the city on one side and the open ocean on the other. On the opposite wall was a fireplace set between two bookcases and surrounded by carved walnut paneling. The bookcases were empty except for one shelf of suspense and detective thrillers. By the window there was a writing table with a pushbutton phone on the top and a filing cabinet beside it. I opened a drawer and dropped the papers into it. A Persian rug, a sofa covered with faded cushions and a couple of upholstered chairs completed the furnishings cozily. With the air of a tour guide, Gus opened a door in the fireplace wall to a bedroom practically filled with a four poster and a matching dresser. The other door revealed a small kitchen equipped with a stove and refrigerator and an antique deal table with two Windsor chairs. The reading lamp and bookstand revealed that Miss Adams liked to read during solitary meals. A miniature television set on a rolling stand told of more frivolous moments. I walked around my new domain opening doors and drawers. Everything was empty and waiting for me to move in.

"This is absolutely enchanting," I said.

"Eh yuh," said Gus Howe. "If you need anything, here's my cell phone number, or you can push the guard button on your desk downstairs." He handed me his card.

"But where is my desk?"

"Right down there in the hall."

"I thought that was Miss Trapper's."

"Nope. She just wishes it were," said Gus and was gone.

I put my belongings away and took a long and welcome shower before changing into my most becoming black suit and proper pumps. Putting on my mother's earrings, I approved of my reflection, which belied the rigors of the drive, and the brief night's sleep. I felt as I often had as a young gymnast before a meet, 'psyched up' for the challenge ahead. The sea wind had brought a rose color to my cheeks and turned my hair into an aureole of curls. My appearance had improved from that of the bedraggled bit of jetsam that had been blown onto the steps of the castle that morning.

After walking across the causeway to a McDonald's on Market Street, I returned to the castle and sat down at the desk opposite the fire, eager to explore my new job. I was pleased to see that the computer was a model familiar to me. I turned it on and perused the files. There was a pile of unopened mail on the blotter. I found a note pad and pen in the top drawer and began a list of questions to ask Miss Adams.

I had been at my desk for perhaps half an hour when the door blew open admitting a gust of cold wind and Jared Fender. I started to my feet. He extended his hand, the pained smile slowly warming his face. "So. The little Athena. What brings you to Brightwater?"

"Hello. Jared." His hand was cold, but his grip firm and muscular. "I work here now. I'm the new curator."

"You? What a strange coincidence."

"What do you mean?"

"Yes. I see." He seemed to be communing more with himself than me. "And what does Emma think?"

"I don't know. I only just met her."

"She wanted this job, but she really doesn't have the background. Never went to the university. Whereas you — I often think of our pleasant evening in New York."

"I'm sure she's wonderful at publicity," I murmured, unaccountably shy. There was no doubt that he was an attractive man.

"Oh yes. Excellent. She is especially busy now, planning the annual fund raising ball, a hundred dollars a head. But you go free, ex officio, and I go because I am a Fender. A hereditary charter member of the university."

"I hadn't heard about it. This is actually my first day — or hour — at the job. I'm still opening mail."

His eyes flickered over me, and he bowed slightly. "Then may I have the honor of your company for the dance?" While I stared, wordless, he rejoined, "Thank you. You are in Miss Adams' rooms?"

At that moment Montero and Emma came in from the cold, exuding camaraderie and martini fumes. "Yes," I said to Jared. "Thank you. I would like that."

"Jared," Montero said, shaking his hand with perfunctory courtesy. Jared's face hardened so that it looked again like a carved mask, behind which his personality seemed to shrink away and efface itself.

"Darling," said Emma. He turned toward her and from behind the mask a single glance flashed and locked with hers as if a spark had arced between them. Then Jared looked again at me, and Emma said, "What brings you here so soon? You're a week early for the dance, Jared."

"You know I would never miss it, Emmy. Also, I had some family business to attend to and I am just back from Brazil and not ready to face New York in this weather. If you don't mind, I'll stroll through the collection."

"Do, please," said Emma. To my mid-western ear, she had a remarkable ability to speak without opening her teeth. "In fact, if the phone rings, do be a perfect lamb and answer it. Monty and I are taking Miss Grey to meet Helen. We'll go in Monty's car. The weather's simply too ghastly for walking."

As we shot back across the causeway, threading the gate like Odysseus's arrow through the axe handles, I clung to the backseat, feeling shy and excluded from their easy companionship.

The hospital stood at the top of the hill next to the university. It was a vaulted old building smelling of disinfectant and years of human misery. A nurse took us to a private room where Miss Adams was propped up, surrounded by white sheets and oxygen tanks. She was small and thin, and with her aquiline nose, shining eyes and short grey hair lying close to her head like feathers, she resembled a sick sea bird. She extended a little curled hand and pulled me close to the bedside, but she spoke first to Emma.

"The printer called about the programs for the ball, Emma. The nurse says that you should use the phone at her station.

There's no cell phone service up here. Monty, would you go downstairs and buy me a box of stationary, plain white letter size?" Her voice was weak but commanding, and they both obeyed as if by habit. The minute we were alone together, she pulled me even closer and whispered with great urgency, "Thank God you've come. Did you get the clipping I sent you?"

"You sent it? I didn't know ..."

"Of course you didn't. But I knew Robert when they were here, years ago. I mailed it to our old friend Mr. Feemster and asked him to forward it, so you wouldn't know it came from Brightwater. Then you might not have come. You are our only hope." She sank back on the pillows, and her breath came hard.

"Shall I call a nurse?"

"No. No. Never join Emma for coffee. They did this to me." She fought for breath again. "The Athena ..."

"Yes?"

"They're trying to steal it."

"Who?"

"Montero. And that old pirate Gus Howe. I overheard them ..." She had to stop again. I heard the sound of high-heeled shoes in the corridor. Her face had grown paler than her hair. I rang for the nurse and bent as close as possible to Miss Adams as Emma came into the room.

"The key to her case," I whispered. "Where is it?"

"There wasn't any phone call, Helen. You were wrong as usual. What are you two whispering about?" said Emma.

"Would you get the nurse right away? I think she's having another attack." To my surprise, Emma obeyed, and I bent closer to Miss Adams.

"The safe. In my room," she gasped.

"What safe? Where?"

Her eyes closed, and her next words were almost inaudible. "Be careful. They got Sophie. They got me. You'll be next."

"Sophie? My mother? Twenty years ago?"

"Feeling sick again? Well, I guess our visit's over." The nurse pushed buttons to lower the pillow and busied herself with her rolling equipment. "Call us later to see how we're doing," she said to me. "Good bye now."

Montero appeared on one side of me and Emma on the other. I felt as if I were in custody. At the door, I looked back quickly. Around the side of the nurse I glimpsed Miss Adams' birdlike face. She winked one shining eye, as if to wish me luck.

Nonetheless, leaving the hospital between my two guards, I heard them talking but was unable to respond. I was trying to absorb what Miss Adams had told me. Montero Courtney was planning to steal the Athena. Yet he and Miss Adams, apparently rivals in some mysterious plot, had both wanted me in Brightwater.

CHAPTER SEVEN

The freezing rain had started up again, more heavily than before while we were inside the hospital, and the parking lot was glazed with ice. I had changed my dress shoes for my salty old boots before leaving the castle, but Emma in her high heels slipped at once and would have fallen if Montero had not caught her.

"Oh dear," she said. "How will we ever get back? We'll probably lose our electricity on Howe's Island — the castle and my poor little house. Gus will be okay. He doesn't have electricity anyway." A gust of wind broke a crystalline branch from a tree nearby and sent it scooting across the ice.

"The car's going to be useless on this hill," Montero said. "And so are your shoes, Emmy. Hang on to me. Athena, can you make it all right?"

"Sure. We get this all the time in Michigan, except out there they salt the streets."

"But not the water. There are those vast fresh water seas. Very strange," he said.

Emma slipped again, almost pulling Montero down with her. I went to her other side and guided her suede glove to the shoulder of my duffle coat. "You have to sort of skate, like this, over to the grass, where we'll get some traction."

"Good idea, Athena. It's less than half a mile down the hill. All set, Emmy?"

Once underway on the grass, she walked more steadily, although parts of the hill were treacherous, especially when a gust of wind blew off the water. At one point I had to grasp a lamp post to steady the three of us. Emma laughed and pressed me momentarily to her scented side. "How nice you are," she exclaimed. "I'm so glad you have come. When Monty said a daughter of the great Robert and Sophie Grey was coming, I pictured a terrifying intellectual."

"Actually," I grinned, "I am a terrifying intellectual."

"Well you don't frighten me — anymore." We reached the bottom of the hill. "I think I can make it on my own ..." But even as she spoke she lost her footing again and resumed her grip on me.

"Lean on me, Grandma," I said, "for I am eight today."

"Little Lord Fauntleroy," she said, delighted. "You're definitely my kind of intellectual. And do you reread *The Secret Garden*?"

"Every year," I said. "At about this time."

"Then you must come and see my garden. It's perfectly divine. I'm your neighbor on Howe's Island, you know, in the old gardener's cottage. It's simply too quaint, all roses and the original estate garden, although some of it has gone a bit wild. I know, Monty! Let's have a dinner party tomorrow, with Athena and Jared.

I think Jared likes you," she added to me, as guilelessly as a teenager. "Come on, Monty. I know you two are like cats and dogs, but we have to stay on good terms with our best dealer."

His only response was a murmured, "Steady" as a new gust blew us to the wall of the causeway. Gus opened the great door for us, and Jared rose from behind my desk. "How's Miss Adams?" he asked.

"She just took a turn for the worse," replied Montero. "Unfortunately, she didn't have time to tell Athena much about the job. And the weather's getting bad out there, Jared. If you were planning to go back to the Fenderbog tonight, you'd better get started." The fire huddled low, sending out a cloud of acrid smoke, and the lights dimmed. Jared shook his watch free of his cuff and recoiled from it.

"It's a simply appalling ice storm," said Emma. "If it hadn't been for Monty and Athena I would be prostrate at the top of College Hill."

"I'd hoped to call on you at the cottage," Jared said.

"Come tomorrow. We're having a dinner party. To welcome Athena." Jared turned his dark gaze on me.

"It will be a pleasure," he said. "Until then, Emma." He kissed her cheek. "Monty." "Jared."

With a perfunctory nod, Jared let himself out, causing another smoky draught to chill the hall.

"I have a four o'clock class," said Montero to me. "But I'll be back later to explain your section of the course. I've been doing it myself since Helen's illness." There was a thud, as if a large shape had struck the battlements. The lights dimmed again.

"You ought to have that goddamned cable laid, Monty," said Gus.

"This summer. For sure. Let's hope the dance is a success. We need the money."

Gus poked up the fire. Montero looked uneasily at the sea outside the east window.

"The electricity on this island," explained Gus to me, "comes over the causeway on a couple wires. Old man Trapper had his own generator, but after it wore out, the city wouldn't pay for a cable when this building was left to the college. I got no power in my place, and Emma's comes from the Castle."

"What happens to the alarm system if the electricity goes off?" I asked.

Gus grinned. "I've got a system of locks, automatically triggered when the electricity goes off. With those things on, nobody gets in, nobody gets out. This castle is the most secure place in North America."

"Gus is the last of the great Yankee inventers," Montero said. "Emmy, I'll walk you home. Gus, would you mind showing Miss Grey around the rest of the castle? I'll be back around five."

"With pleasure," Gus said as the door banged and the fire shuddered again. "I hire and train the other guards, mostly college kids or local boys. We rotate the shifts, so none of us always gets the night watch."

"How long have you worked here?" I asked.

"I took over from my Pa in 1965, when he retired. Before he worked for the college, he worked for old man Trapper, driving his car, sailing his boat."

"His boat?"

"A three masted schooner, like the one on the Canadian dime. They used to run out of Gloucester and from Halifax to Savannah. Beautiful boats. One of Mr. Trapper's businesses, in fact his best money maker, was shipping produce from here to Boston and New York." He raised an eyebrow and gave me an amused look, which I didn't understand, before turning toward the staircase to the gallery.

"You must have been very young," I said.

"Sixteen. Old enough to quit school. Not that I didn't like school. I did, and I was good at it. But I needed the job. My old man was fifty when I was born, and my mother died young."

We had reached the top of the stairs and stood looking down the vista of the old ballroom toward the Athena. "There she is. The prize of the collection."

"How ..." To my chagrin, I found it hard to keep my voice steady, lightly conversational, because of the pounding of my heart. "How did the Trapper family first acquire it?"

"Old man Trapper used to tell us how he dug it up in Greece all by himself, Miss Grey." "Athena. Please."

"Okay. If you call me Gus." He offered me his hand, as if clinching a bargain, and I shook it. "But he was able to use her, because of all the gold, don't you know, as collateral, to finance his first legitimate business, Trapper Mills in New Stoke, when he was first starting out, so's you might say she founded the family fortune.

He got half this island off my father in a crooked deal with the bank. What's left, my part of the island, I hold under a charter from King Charles the Second. I hope someday to get the rest back. Did I tell you that old man Trapper was a rascal?" He endowed the old fashioned epithet with more contempt than could have been expressed by any obscenity.

"No. But I could guess."

"Well, he was. Anyway, he built this castle and the causeway on our island and did a lot of traveling, bringing back all this stuff, fancy furniture and rugs and pictures and statues."

"Now they all belong to the university," I said.

"That's right. Old Man Trapper left the house and all to the college because he was in trouble with his taxes. Just like Al Capone." Again he raised his eyebrow. "All except the Athena. He wanted that kept in the family, so it's loaned to the museum, but it belongs to poor Emma."

"And Emma's the only family member left?"

"Eh-yuh. Mr. Trapper married late, handsome girl, but no background. They say she was a showgirl. Their only son drank himself to death young, and Emma was his only child."

He led me into the grand salon with its Chinese rug and collection of early renaissance paintings. In the great dining room, portraits by Rembrandt and Van Dyke stared down at a table set with gold goblets and plates made for the Medici. "You see how the other half lives," said Gus. There was another thud, and he cocked his head, listening. A brief hum of electricity gone awry was followed by dimness and then darkness.

"Goddamn it to hell," Gus said mildly. "I've got to go, Athena. Here." He flicked on a zippo, which flared like a torch, and lit the five candles of a candelabrum on the sideboard. Our shadows stalked crazily across the wall as he handed the candles to me. "We'll have to finish the tour later. I've got to check my locks. Nice talking to you. Come and see me at my house on the island. You'd be royally entertained." He was off down one of the passages in silence and darkness.

"Thanks, Gus," I called after him. "I'd like that."

"Bye now." The foghorn voice seemed to echo from a great distance.

I made my way back to the hall, where, although night had not fallen, the storm made it too dark to work. I turned off my lifeless computer and unplugged it. Black smoke streamed from my candles as I mounted the great staircase and then the smaller one to my tower room, where I set my candles on my writing table. I shivered in the damp air, and it took me a long time to kindle the fire which had been laid on my hearth. The wind moaned and sobbed in the chimney. I went to a window seat and wrapped my arms around my knees, leaning my forehead against the cold glass. The sea below was black as oil. I was locked into the castle and alone. The only meal I had eaten since Ann Arbor was a McDonald's hamburger.

Determined to avoid the abyss of self-pity and exhaustion over which I hovered, I focused my thoughts on the events of the day. I had finally seen the Athena. And discovered that it was supposed to belong to Emma Trapper, although it had been bequeathed to me, or rather the papers which established its authenticity belonged to me. If indeed it was a solid gold and ivory replica rather than a fifth century B.C. masterpiece, as Montero Courtney's book had argued, it was certainly valuable, although not a major monument, not worth millions of dollars to Mr. Bartholomew Badger.

Darkness was falling, and the candles cast strange wavering shapes on the carved woodwork. My situation, which had seemed so simple in the clear electric light of Michigan, had here in the shadows of Brightwater become a mystery into which my mind seemed to sink as slowly but inexorably as the piers of the Fenderbog Bridge sank into the tidal rip of the canal.

I thought about Emma, my rival. I had tried to cast her as the stereotypical villain of my story, gorgeous but repulsive; but once I had grown accustomed to her eastern boarding school way of talking, she had revealed herself as genuinely pleasant to be with, affectionate and enthusiastic, if perhaps, not too bright. And still gorgeous. *And, face it, you said it yourself: the rival. The responsibility.* I furiously rubbed my eyes and noticed that my hands were sooty from the fire. The thought of how I might look made me suddenly giggle. Just then there was a knock on my door.

"Gus! Thank God! I was afraid I would starve here." But the figure that filled the doorway was not Gus. It was Montero Courtney with a shopping bag in his arms. His quick smile flashed.

"I'm sorry I'm not Gus, but you won't starve." He set the bag down on my table and hung his oilskin jacket on the back of the chair, where it dripped on the floor. He was wearing a navy issue black turtleneck sweater and jeans. "Are you all right? You're so pale."

"Not surprising," I answered wryly. "You could have warned me before you just appeared dressed like a cat burglar."

"Suitable to the occasion. I came to show you some real cat burglar stuff." He stopped abruptly, looking at me keenly in the candlelight. "But, what's happened to your face?"

"My hands got all dirty, making the fire."

He drew out a linen handkerchief, dampened it on the shoulder of his oilskins, and cradling my chin in his hand, wiped the soot from my face. I held myself stiffly, almost drawing back, for the touch of his hand had brought back all too vividly the fierce sweetness of those minutes in the driveway at Oakhill. He put his handkerchief back in his pocket, but for a moment his hand moved across my cheek in a caress as light as a breeze, the kind of breeze that will fan dormant coals into blazing fires. I stepped back, as if from the heat of such a fire. He smiled. "Better now?"

"Yes. Thanks. I was a little depressed at the thought of being locked in here."

"I thought you might be. That's why I came. There is a way out, but only Gus and I know about it. I'm about to make you the third party to the secret." He blew out the candles and unhooked a flashlight from his belt and switched it on, throwing a circle of light in an arc around the room. "You'll need a jacket." I took my windbreaker out of my closet. "Follow me."

In the hall he walked as silently as a shadow, close to the wall, down the stairs and into the breakfast room which adjoined the main dining room. It was in one of the back towers, and the flashlight beam showed that it was half circular, like my room. The wind hummed in the window casements.

"Now watch this," he said. "I've heard that there's more than one, but this is the only one that Gus and I know about for sure." He led me out of the tower again and into the corner of the big dining room. "You know how your room has that little kitchen behind it? Well, this one has a butler's pantry and a dumbwaiter." He showed me the narrow room filled with shelves and the sliding door to the dumbwaiter. "Notice the dumbwaiter doesn't fill its chute."

We went back to the tower, and Montero took a ship model from the mantelpiece and placed it on the table. He pressed a knot in the paneling, and one of the china cupboards gave a little click and swung open like a door. On its back were shelves, empty now except for a few dusty bottles of whiskey and brandy. Behind it was a passage of stone from which a clammy draft blew.

"Spooky, isn't it?" said Montero." "Stay close to me now."

I held back for a minute, repelled as if the passage exuded some anti-magnetic force. The memory of Miss Adams' sharp whisper, "Montero and that old pirate Gus Howe" flashed through my mind. I set my teeth and stepped behind the cupboard.

The air was so chill and damp that it was almost unbreathable. I coughed. There was a tiny circular staircase, and after the first turn I was descending into darkness. A cobweb brushed my cheek, and I felt its occupant on my neck. "Monty? Are you there?" My voice echoed, thin and quavering, back from the cold rocks.

He took my hand and held it for the rest of the dark, dizzying way down. At the bottom he directed the beam of the flashlight to a rough door secured by a crossbar set into rusty brackets. From the other side I could hear the sigh and wash of the sea. He removed the bar and pushed the door, which responded with a groan. The hair stirred on the back of my neck. Montero pushed again, and again the door creaked. "I'll help you," I said and forced the door until it yielded enough to let us through. The next passage was narrow and smelled strongly of seaweed and clams. The flashlight revealed that the walls were of slate, salty and wet.

"Well done," said Montero. "You're strong for your size."

"Thanks. I used to be a gymnast." A splash of icy water fell on my head, and I tasted salt on my lips. The rocks that formed three steps down were slimy, and I was grateful for his hand. "Is this a natural cave?"

"Some of it must be. Undercut by the tide, probably. Here we are." It was another door like the first, but easier to open. It led into a spacious stone chamber where the scent and sound of the sea were very strong. Against the wall beside me leaned several pairs of oars. Coiled lines and life preservers, faded and moldy, hung on pegs around the periphery. Pulled up on a ramp before us was a clinker-built workboat.

"The old boathouse," said Montero. He led me forward, down the ramp beside the boat to a window next to the double doors at the front of the boathouse. He unboarded it, and the northeast wind blew in, cold but fresh and sweet after the dreadful air of the passages behind us.

Against the night sky we could see the Brightwater Bridge across the dark harbor. To our right, the city of Brightwater, studded with lighted windows, rose from the wharves and pilings of the waterfront, with the floodlighted spire of the church halfway up the hill and the gothic turrets of the university crowning the Point. On the other, the ramp extended into the sea. The ebbing tide had left bare the seaweed and barnacles at the end. High tide must come nearly to the boathouse door, I thought.

"During Prohibition," Montero said, "the rumrunners used to bring the stuff in here and up the secret passageway right into the house, direct from the ships anchored off the three mile limit. From there they would take it out the Fenderbog Road to Boston and New York."

Something jogged my memory. What was it? I shivered.

"You're cold," he said. "Come on back and I'll treat you to dinner." He led the way back up the slimy staircase, and I drew a breath of relief when I rounded the last turn and stepped out into the relative warmth of the breakfast room.

Back in my own sitting room. I lighted the candles again, and the night stepped back behind the big window, turning it into a mirror, which gave back our reflections in chiaroscuro, like figures in a Caravaggio painting.

Montero knelt on the hearth, spreading the hot coals evenly. Then he reached into his shopping bag and drew out a small grill on legs, which he placed over the fire. Next came a black iron frying pan wrapped in aluminum foil, which on being opened revealed potatoes already peeled and cut up, mixed with butter.

Placed on half the grill, it began to sizzle. I suddenly felt almost faint with hunger.

"Sit down," he said, and as I sank into the window seat, he produced a bottle of red wine, uncorked it, and poured some into two glasses which he found in Miss Adams' kitchen. The next foray into the bag produced a porterhouse steak, which soon joined the potatoes on the grill, and a bowl of salad which he placed on my table.

"How wonderful," I said. "You're like Mr. Micawber, saving the day by cooking a grill in the fireplace."

He turned the steak over, and the fire flared and lighted his intent face. His heavy hair, now falling over his forehead, was touched with grey, but his unguarded expression made him seem younger than the authoritative figure who during the day had dominated the college museum.

"You don't look like Mr. Micawber," I added. "More like David himself." I had meant it only lightly, in the sense that he was the hero of the current adventure, but his face abruptly darkened.

"Yes. Too much so. This time you seem to be the clairvoyant." He turned away and busied himself bringing plates and silver from the kitchen, and even after he had placed the table with its little feast in front of the window seat and sat down beside me, he remained silent.

Near starvation was stronger than my concern for my companion. The steak was beautifully cooked, red within and lightly charred, with the rare, true taste of hardwood coals. The salad was so good that when I had finished mine I could not resist a glance at the plate of Montero, who still seemed immersed in gloomy thoughts. "Are you going to finish yours?" I asked.

"What? Oh. Take what you need." His smile flashed, and he began to eat again. Finally replete, we leaned back on the cushions to finish our wine.

"This was kind of you," I said.

"Well, I didn't think it was right to let you be locked in here alone, especially on your first night. At least now you know how to escape if you have to."

"Escape?" I said. "That's a funny way of putting it."

"Only realistic, Athena. You know that as long as you have the papers with you, you are never out of very real danger. Ned O'Neill called me today to make sure that you had arrived safely and had carried out your father's last wish and given them to me."

The mention of a last wish brought forcefully to my mind all my doubts of the evening as well as my visit to Miss Adams and her frantic, whispered warning. Our eyes met for a long time, and I felt as if I were sinking beneath a feeling of profound sadness and loneliness. "I don't mean to frighten you," he said, "but I must have the papers. Now."

I began to stall for time, and turned away so that he could not read my face. "If the doors all lock automatically," I said, "and the only way in is through the boathouse, how did you get in during such a storm?"

"I never left. I keep a few things here in one of the spare bedrooms so that I can stay overnight in case of a power failure or I have been working late and the causeway is flooded or iced over."

"How did you manage this beautiful feast?" I turned back and smiled at him. There was pride in his answering smile.

"I raided the big kitchen downstairs. The steak was left over from a business conference last weekend. Those executives really know how to eat."

"Luckily for me," I said.

"Where are they?"

I lied outright, inspired by the fortress in which we were trapped. "They are locked in the trunk of my car," I said, "where, except for when Ned O'Neill had them, I've kept them since the night my father died. Is there any way we can get to them now?"

"Not until either the electricity goes on or the tide goes out. It's flowing now. The rest of the island can only be reached from the boathouse at dead low tide."

From my quick glance at the boathouse, I had suspected as much. I was relieved to have bought a little time to ponder my situation. He reached out and touched my hair, turning a curl on the back of neck around his fingers. Then he abruptly drew back, as if from an electric shock. He started to his feet.

"Well, there we are. I'll pick them up from you tomorrow. It will be a sad occasion without Robert, but also a great one. We should celebrate. Would you like to come out to our house at Bluecove for lunch? My Uncle William, you father's professor, will be there. He has waited a long time for this day."

I had a sudden memory, as clear as a vision. I was back in Agios Titos with William Courtney and the nephew Montero, who so strongly resembled him. Monty was a boy of sixteen, but to me he was a grown-up, and he had just asked William if he could borrow his boat and take me for a sail. I remembered the harbor and the water, that indescribable shade of Aegean blue. I remembered feeling a little shy at first, but then talking easily about his home back in Brightwater. He told me that it was even more beautiful than Agios Titos. After we had sailed around the harbor, we tied up at the little dock and walked together to the village museum. He was so much taller than I that I had to hold on to the leg of his jeans to keep up with him. We walked out of the dazzling sunshine and into the cool shadows of the little museum and stood before an empty niche for a while before returning to the little taverna where my mother, father and William Courtney were drinking wine and eating dolmades and spanakopita. They ordered me a ngazoza, and I joined them at the table, feeling that this had been the best day of my entire life, all of six years. The vision of that afternoon in Greece had beguiled my dreams, both sleeping and waking, for the last twenty years. I longed to meet William Courtney again, but I worried about my professional obligations.

"I'm not sure that Emma can spare me ..."

"Emma would agree," he said, and his face was suddenly so grim that I, too, stood up and moved a little away from him. He loaded the empty containers into his shopping bag. I didn't want him to go.

"We never got around to talking about your course," I said.

"We can do that at lunch," he said, preoccupied, still frowning. He opened the door and turned back to me before picking up his possessions. "But there was something else we were talking about. I forget. Was it important?"

"David Copperfield?"

"Oh yes. And your clairvoyance." He picked up the shopping bag and stood framed in the doorway.

"You overestimate my powers. I don't understand."

"Don't you? Remember that devastating line? 'There can be no disparity in marriage like unsuitability of mind and purpose.' Good night, Athena. Open the door for nobody."

"Good night, Montero."

The door closed and he was gone.

CHAPTER EIGHT

    I locked the door and pulled down the shades on all my windows and tucked them in carefully at the sides. Then I crossed softly to the fireplace. It was surrounded by varnished walnut carved in a design of leaves and fruit. Above the mantelpiece there was a panel, in the center of which hung an old painting of Harbor Street with an arcaded market and cows grazing nearby and Howe's Island in the background. It would be typical of Alfred Trapper's taste in architecture, I thought, to have hidden a safe behind the panel with a catch hidden in the carving — something out of a 1920's mystery novel, like the secret passage to the boathouse. I ran my hands along the carving at the bottom of the panel feeling for a spring.

    My shoulders began to ache. The ticking of the clock on the mantel seemed loud in the silence. I put it on the desk and looked at the square in the dust where it had stood. There was a small knot in the wood, but when I pressed it, nothing happened.

    My eyes felt hot and sandy. The wind buffeted the building in gusts and now and then drew a howling sound from the chimney that caused the hair on my arms to stand up. I could hear the distant surf and, nearer, the high tide splashing at the ledges below the castle. I rubbed my eyes and pushed the hair back from my forehead and resumed probing the paneling.

Above the noises of the night I heard the sound of footsteps in the corridor outside my room, and I froze like a hunted rabbit. The measured tread came nearer and nearer and then stopped, as if listening outside my door. I heard the sound of someone breathing. In a minute the footsteps began again, and the sound faded away down the corridor. I breathed again and moved my desk chair under the doorknob, but it was too low to reach, so I moved it to the fireplace and stood on it to reach the top of the paneling. As I ran my hands along the carving, I touched an acorn, which yielded to pressure. I turned and pressed and wiggled it, but to no avail. I was just about to give up when, in response to downward pressure, it gave a click. The painting swung outward and opened a little safe. I reached my hand in and closed it over the cool metal of a key.

I shut the safe with a sound that seemed to echo through the castle, even over the noise of the wind. I got down from the chair, and, driven by an impulse I couldn't control, I slipped off my shoes and blew out the candles and tiptoed to the door.

The corridor was chill and silent and very dark. I found my way by feeling along the wall as I crept downstairs toward the gallery. There I could see a little as my eyes grew accustomed to the dark. The Athena was visible against the window by the dim light of the night sky.

I moved toward her as silently as possible. I had no idea what I intended to do after I tried the key, but I felt around for the keyhole in front of the case. The key fitted and moved slowly in the lock, but when I tried to lift the case, I found that it was too big and heavy even for my gymnast's strength. I decided to come back by daylight. But when I tried to close the case I found that the catch had jammed open and would not close again. In the darkness it was impossible to see or correct the problem. I wiggled the key and couldn't remove it from the lock.

Once again I heard the footsteps approaching.

My hands were so sweaty that I couldn't get a good enough grip on the key to wrench it loose. I looked around for a place to hide and saw the velvet curtains by the window. I started toward them, but a loose board in the parquet floor groaned under my foot. I heard the footsteps stop.

I realized that, against the window, I must be more visible than the statue. I quickly slipped behind the curtain. It sighed and swayed and released a quantity of dust. I felt a sneeze coming. I held my nose.

The footsteps began again. They were coming directly toward me. A gleam of light shone on the floor and moved by, pausing in front of the statue. I strained to hear more, but the sneeze had dulled my hearing. The light began to move again, turning and going off to the right. It seemed an eternity before it traversed the second floor and descended the stairs and disappeared around a corner.

I slipped out of my hiding place and approached the case of the Athena again. I felt along the bottom crack. It was tightly closed. I felt the keyhole. It was empty. The key was gone.

Crestfallen, I retraced my steps back to my room. I lit the candles and looked quickly around, but my things appeared undisturbed. I locked the door and went immediately to my file cabinet, where the metal box still lay in the drawer.

Standing on the chair to open the safe, I fitted my father's box in with some difficulty. It had to be stood on its side. I shut the little door and started nervously at the click of the lock.

Suddenly the lights went on and the refrigerator began to hum. The telephone lights were on, three of them, one for the outside line and two inside lines. Someone else was in the castle that night besides Montero and me. I picked up the receiver, but the lights went off in quick succession, and when I listened there was nobody there.

Finally aware in every bone and muscle of the long day and short night behind me, I got ready for bed. In spite of the wind and the surf, I fell asleep almost at once.

The storm had blown out to sea when I went down to my desk the following morning. The sunlight sparkled on the tracery of ice on the tree branches outside the window, and brightness glittered in the air.

I had expected to hear from Montero immediately, and I had run out of ideas for ways of holding back the papers. I had awakened during the night to realize that it would be ultimately impossible to avoid the terms of my father's will. Certainly in our short friendship Montero had shown me nothing but kindness.

Every kindness except trust. But, after all, our distrust was mutual.

In any case, I was disappointed and then angry to find myself alone in the great hall, staring at a strange computer, uncertain of my duties. I became determined to find a way to speak to Miss Adams again. Alone. As soon as possible. There was a great deal she could tell me. Certainly nobody else would.

It was nearly nine when the front door opened, but it admitted only Emma Trapper. "Monty won't be coming in today," she said. "He has no Wednesday classes anyway, and I suppose there is a lot to be done at a big place like Bluecove after a storm like yesterday's. But isn't it beautiful now? Too divine a day to be trapped by the telephone, but I'm waiting for a call from a band about the dance. Athena, darling, you're going to have plenty to do starting tomorrow, what with the Parthenon lecture in the evening and the dance on Saturday. Why don't you take the day off? Explore Howe's Island and the Point"

"That's very kind of you," I said, "but I'm afraid I don't even know what the Parthenon lecture is, never mind what I am supposed to do."

"Oh, my poor poppet. Monty has certainly been neglecting you. He can be a perfect beast with his assistants. You must come to me and complain the minute he makes you unhappy. The Parthenon lecture is part of the college's Western Civ. Program. Every week one of the professors gives a varsity lecture required of all freshmen, but everyone goes because it's in the evening and it's fun — sort of a star turn except when old Herr Graubart does Goethe and nobody can understand a WORD he's saying, not even the German department who assume he is speaking English, which he's not..." Emma paused and drew breath. "Where was I?"

"The Parthenon lecture."

"Oh. Yes. Well, Monty's annual tour de force is Thursday night— tomorrow — and the lecture hall is always jammed, not just university people but Old Brightwater in serried ranks, even more people turn out for the dance, old fossils from Bluecove and the Fenderbog. Of course, he's the darling of the Point, related to all the founding families, the Howes, the Fenders, the Courtneys, and famous, too, and he's a born ham. His mother was an actress you know, Maude Montero before she married Judge Courtney and retired from the New York stage. Now she positively dominates both the Brightwater Reparatory and the Brightwater Light Opera."

"Of course. I had heard the name, but I didn't know there was a connection." Maude Montero had not only dominated the stage for several years but had starred in several movies before she had retired to this small city because, according to the tabloids, she did not want to raise her children in Hollywood.

"Anyway, he knocks 'em dead. Pulls out all stops and ends up passionate about the return of the Elgin Marbles. He's quite mad on the subject of the theft of the Greek national treasures. Has been all his life."

"Have you known him all his life?"

"Well, all of mine anyway. He and Jared are a little older than I am, but we all grew up together, playing in Trapper's Castle and sailing with Gus Howe and listening to his yarns and his father's experiences running rum." Her voice trailed off, oddly wistful and stripped of its affectations as her unfocussed gaze viewed the distances of the past. "It was lovely to be a child in Brightwater." She gave herself a little shake. "Much nicer than being a grown-up, to be honest. This place can stifle you. Everyone knows everyone else and all their family history since the Flood. No mistake is ever forgotten, no wrongdoing is ever forgiven. Sometimes I think I should get away, start a whole new life. But go along, Athena. Enjoy it while you can, while it is still new to you and beautiful."

"Thanks, Emma."

Everywhere outdoors there was the sound of water dripping off the towers, and the nostalgic breeze was soft with the scent of bare earth and new growth. I turned my face to the sun, closing my eyes against the brightness. It was too nice a day to drive. I would walk to the hospital and find Miss Adams.

The sound of a footstep caused me to open my eyes. Before me, bending his dark head courteously, stood Jared Fender. "We meet again, Athena. What brings you out on this beautiful morning?"

"Emma suggested that I explore the surroundings since she has to stay by the telephone."

"What a lovely idea. I wish I could be your guide, but I have business with Emma. And I will have the pleasure of seeing you this evening. May I call for you at six? Emma usually dines early. Brightwater is very much a provincial city." The pained smile briefly warmed his face. "Until then." He drew his heels together and took my hand in his. The breeze stirred the lapel of his blazer and then blew it open, revealing a silver and pearl handled pistol in a shoulder holster. I drew my hand back, but he held it more firmly. "What is it, my dear? Your hand is so cold. Oh. My artillery. Surely it doesn't alarm you that, since I have to carry priceless treasures through New York every day, I am prepared to protect myself. There. That's better." The breeze blew my hair over my forehead, and, with his free hand, he brushed it back, turning a curl over one finger. From the top of a nearby tree a cardinal poured out its manic mating song. Jared turned my hand over and examined the palm for a minute and then looked back into my eyes before curling my fingers closed and returning my hand to me as if it were a gift.

"Do you read hands as well as minds?" I asked as coolly as I could.

"Yes. And yours is as enchanting as your mind," he said and was gone, the door of the castle swinging shut behind him.

I waited a minute to allow my heartbeat to return to normal, not sure whether it raced because of his weapon or the same physical magnetism that I had felt in New York. Then I descended the steps and set out across the causeway and up the hill, far different in the April sunshine than it had been in the storm of the day before.

Miss Adams was doing better this morning, the nurse at the station told me, and would surely welcome a visitor.

"There! I knew it! I knew you would come back," Miss Adams chirped. She cocked her head and laid down a paperback adorned with an excessively well-built young woman fleeing a building all too similar to Trapper's Castle. "Sit down, sit down, Athena."

I took the chair next to the bed. "I'm so glad you're better," I said, "because I haven't had a chance to ask you about all kinds of things." I took out my notebook, and her birdlike manner changed to a cool professionalism as she briskly answered all my questions and added considerable information that I hadn't known enough to ask for.

We must have talked for nearly an hour, for she grew tired suddenly, in the manner of an invalid, and leaned back on her pillow with a sigh.

"I've worn you out," I said. "I'm sorry. Shall I call the nurse?"

"Oh no. Heavens no. She is in on it, too. With Emma. Don't ever have coffee with Emma. She poisons people. She poisoned me."

I looked at the open door, hoping to see a nurse pass by.

"She's in on it, with Monty and Gus, you see. Until you came, I was the only one trying to stop their plot. That's why I hid the key."

"Their plot?"

"I told you. Stealing the Athena. They had to do it soon. Before Robert was finished. That's why they murdered Robert." She leaned forward again, but her glassy eyes seemed to look beyond me.

"You see, Robert's research would have ruined Monty's professional reputation. You know how these professors are. All egomaniacs. Besides, they could fence a solid gold replica, but not a major monument."

"But surely..."

She laid her little claw on my hand. "Oh yes, Athena. Even Jared says so. And Jared knows everything about the art market." Her grip tightened as I leaned across her to press the nurse button, and she gave a little cry. "Don't! You're in it, too. Oh, you're one of them. Oh, and I thought I could trust you."

"Please, Miss Adams." I patted her awkwardly and she grew calm again, leaning back on the pillow, suddenly drowsy. "They're all around us, you know. Everywhere. We're never safe." She slept.

As I stared, the nurse arrived. "Off again, are we? Well, but she was pretty alert there for a while, wasn't she? That's how it goes. Perfectly lucid one minute, and the next? Paranoid. Or sometimes one of her ghost stories. She's a one, isn't she, with her imagination?"

"Is she... "

"It's not for me to say. They're still testing, but it looks like a chemical reaction. Psychosis from poison, like."

"Poison."

"Like medication. These old timers. You just never know. Well, call us later, Miss, and we'll let you know how she's doing."

Rehearsing this odd interlude in my mind as I walked down the hill and across the causeway, I was so bemused that I did not realize that I was being hailed until I heard my name called a second time.

"Athena! Ahoy there!"

I knew only one person capable of saying "Ahoy" without affectation. I spotted Gus, and, turning, I walked to the iron gate that barred access to the castle from the rest of the island. It was unlocked, and I let myself out to the cobblestone street which ran along the seawall.

Gus and his boat were on the sand between the high water line and a ramp from the seawall, built for the launching of small boats. He raised his hand to the visor of his cap when he saw me, and I went to his side and joined him in admiration of the hull, freshly caulked and painted with copper. "Smooth as a baby's bottom," said Gus. "Just about ready to go over, but I got to fix the handgrip on the tiller. Come on in and join me, Athena. It's a good day for visiting. I'd like you to see my house. I have this land on a charter from King Charles the Second, since Elizabeth Howe came here the same year as Sir Peter Fender, way back when."

"I would like that," I said, walking with him across the street to the seventeenth century house, its shingles weathered to silver by centuries of wind-driven salt and sand.

His parlor, dominated by a large fireplace and furnished with sofa and chairs of carved rosewood and black horsehair, was as tidy as a ship's cabin. Behind it, the kitchen was heated by a shipmate stove set on the hearth, its brass guardrail polished. Passing the sink and drain board cut from one great slab of slate and dominated by a hand pump, Gus opened a wooden Icebox and chipped several chunks from a block of ice with an ice pick. He divided them between two jelly glasses and took a bottle of whiskey down from an open shelf. "Join me, Athena?"

I hesitated for the duration of a heartbeat, and he grinned and filled his own glass. "Being the commodore of this island, I say when the sun clears the yardarm." I smiled back, and he filled my glass and led me across the kitchen floor, the slope of which caused me to lurch slightly before I had even tasted my drink. "I think we can sit out," he said. "Looks like the first good day for sitting out since Thanksgiving."

The back door led to a porch overlooking a lawn washed with the first green of spring, although a little snow remained in the shadow of the stone wall which surrounded it. Beyond the wall, I could see the harbor and part of the city, but directly in front of us the ocean lay blue and smooth but rising and falling with the groundswell, like the breathing of the sleeping earth. Gus drew a rocking chair forward and held it for me before settling himself on his own chair on the other side of the round wicker table.

"Cheers," he said, and we clinked glasses and drank. He reached into his pocket and drew out a bundle of tarred line and a jack knife. "Hand me that marlin spike, would you?" He jerked his head toward a sort of heavy wooden ice pick on the porch rail beside me.

"This?"

"Eh-yuh."

"Here."

"And that tiller in the corner." The shaft of varnished wood was leaning against the house wall. It was worn smooth by salt and sand, and the grip of braided string at the end was frayed to ravelings.

"It's heavy," I said.

"Solid oak," nodded Gus, laying it across the table. He opened his knife and began to remove the remains of the handgrip. "Belongs to my catboat, which I have from my grandfather. Twenty feet overall. You'd never think a boat that size would sleep two below with a stove and a chart table and plenty of stowage besides, would you?"

I composed my features in an expression of suitable amazement.

"Nah," said Gus. "They don't build them like they used to. Racing machines, that's what they want, or a fiberglass tub, no maintenance, take the wife and kids out on a Sunday drive. Nah."

I sipped my drink and shook the glass to hear the ice jingle.

"That's good ice," said Gus. "Comes from Jack's fish store, down Point's End. He still gets it off Courtney's Pond in the winter, just like he always did. I don't have a power line down here. Don't need one. Just makes you dependent. Might as well be one of those folks on the hill. You see what happens at the castle."

I didn't know who the folks on the hill were, but I assumed that they had grown effete from overdependence on nineteenth century technology.

"Can you sail your boat alone?" I asked, intrigued by this vision of independence.

"Eh-yuh. That's what she's made for. She's got a lot of sail, but with your gaff rig, you can take the wind or spill it. My old man could run a heavy cargo up to long island in that old cat, fifty knot gale, four inches of free board." His gnarled brown hands manipulated phantom halyards in the air. "You could raise your peak or drop it, get a big belly in that sail. She could have carried another five hundred pounds."

"What cargo?" I asked politely. Gus was shaken by a silent chuckle.

"Well, you know it wasn't oysters in them days. Before Repeal. And they had to go out in weather so bad that the feds couldn't follow." He peeled the last bit of string from the tiller and stroked it, rubbing off the sand that had accumulated underneath. "I wasn't born then, but the old timers used to talk about those days." He took up the coil of string and began to weave it deftly around the end of the tiller with the marlin spike. "But that's the way it's always been on the Point, back to the days when Brightwater was a port for the pirate ships, or when they brought tea and opium back from China in the prettiest vessels ever built. The Fenders built that big place of theirs on money they made as wreckers, building bonfires so's masters of merchant ships would take them for the Squanocket Point Light and run aground on Point's End. The other families mostly went to sea. So when Prohibition came along, it was like reviving an old local industry. Christ, even the Indians and the Gypsies was running rum down the Fenderbog Road to Boston. And old man Trapper?" He grinned at me with raised eyebrows. "When it comes to the old families on the Point, the question isn't were they pirates and smugglers. They all were. It's that some were good guys and some were bad guys."

"Tell me about the Fenders," I said. He paused, spike in hand.

"Very peculiar family," he said at length. "There's too much to tell in one sitting."

"About Jared then."

"He's not a Fender," Gus said shortly. "He's a Courtney."

"What do you mean?"

"Jared's mother Veronica, who later married Si Fender, was — is - the handsomest woman the Point ever saw, and we got some handsome women. Look at Maude Montero. Anyway, Veronica, she came from an old Indian family, her grandfather was the chief of the Squanockets, but that's another story. They had married into other families, Frenchmen, Irishmen, Veronica's own mother was part Gypsy, but they kept their identity as Indians. Veronica's father died young, killed in a hunting accident. She is still so handsome that there's old timers, me included, that'll stop what they're doing just to watch her pass by. Well, thirty some years ago, she got engaged to Will Courtney. Monty's uncle. Famous archeologist."

"Yes," I said. "He was my father's boss once."

"But shortly after, he went off to Greece on one of his archeology trips, was supposed to come back and get married in a month or so." He stopped his work with the marlin spike and laid his hands down on the table, looking out to sea and blinking rapidly.

"Yes?" I prompted.

He cleared his throat. "Word came back... word came back that he had been killed. By communist bandits. The mountains of Greece were full of them at that time. Right away Veronica married Silas Fender, almost as if it was arranged by the family. I guess it was. Silas was old enough to be Veronica's father. In fact, some of us thought he had been sweet on Veronica's mother, Ursula, used to read palms and tell fortunes down at an amusement park before it was washed away by a hurricane."

My head was beginning to swim. "There sure are a lot of stories on the Point," I said. Gus's eyes were still fixed on the horizon, misty, as if he were reading a sad story written somewhere out there in the blue haze where sea met sky.

"Jared was born seven months later," he said. "The next year Will turned up, lame but alive. He'd been rescued and nursed back to health by some villagers. Too late for Veronica. The worst of it was that Si Fender was the meanest man ever born. Fine looking fellow, but mean. He's mellowed some, being crippled and all, but in those days he was." Gus picked up the tiller and resumed his weaving. "They say he hadn't always been that way. I guess he was a nice enough kid. One of the smart Fenders. Went to Harvard. But after his old man up and married the widow Ursula."

"I'll say, they are a peculiar family," I burst out. "But then weren't Veronica and Silas Fender stepsister and brother?"

"Silas's father married Madam Ursula after their kids were married, although not long after." Gus saw no humor in the story. "Really surprised the Point, old Fender being like a hermit, all wrapped up in his books and never going out. Anyway, living in the house with Ursula all those years kind of twisted Si all up. And after Jared was born Si just got even meaner. Used to beat Veronica and the boy. Couldn't miss the resemblance, I guess. All the Courtneys look alike. Although it's funny. Jared doesn't have the smile. Guess there wasn't much to smile about. When he was sixteen, he shot Silas. Didn't kill him, but Si's been in a wheelchair ever since. Madam Ursula was injured in the same accident and died a few weeks later. Monty's father, judge Courtney, dead now, ruled it an accident but saw that Jared was sent off to boarding school somewhere out in the Midwest. He was a clever young fellow. That's how the Fenders are. Half are simple. Half are geniuses. The inbreeding, I guess. I hear he's doing all right in New York. He has some good luck coming to him, I guess." Gus sat for a while in silence, then emptied his glass in one draught.

"It's been hard for him all his life," he resumed presently. "Growing up in that great wreck of a house, abused by that rascal Si Fender, seeing the Courtney's all so happy at Bluecove. Look across

Howe's Harbor there. You can see it from here. The garden spot of the Point."

I followed his gaze across the water. Between the city and the promontory at the southernmost tip of the little cape I could see a calm inlet below a stretch of woodland and lawn and, visible even from this distance of perhaps a half mile a rambling white house with many chimneys. "Seems the sun always shines at Bluecove. I could never see why he didn't hate them. But he grew up on the shore here, running in and out of all the houses with Monty and Emmy. The Point's a good place for kids. But those days are gone, Athena. Yessiree, gone forever. Well, got to keep going anyway." He laid the tiller on the table and heaved himself stiffly to his feet. "Can I get you a refill, Athena?"

"No thanks, Gus. I'm still working on this one."

He disappeared into his kitchen, where I heard him chipping ice and pouring whiskey before he settled again into his chair. "You know, Athena, I'm not an educated man. I had to quit school when I was sixteen to go to work for old man Trapper."

"Your father had died?"

"Lost at sea. Put out in that same boat, somehow got washed overboard. The boat was found the next day drifting."

"I'm sorry."

"Nice of you. Guess you know how it feels. But I ain't sure he didn't go willingly. It was about a year since Old Man Trapper got most of his land and ruined him."

His eyes were fixed on the horizon for so long that I gently prompted him, "You were saying that you regretted leaving school."

He gave a little start and resumed his work on the handgrip. "Eh-yuh. But I read a lot, down here alone nights with my Aladdin lamp. Even keep up with my high school Latin. And I enjoy talking with Will Courtney. He comes sailing and fishing with me a lot. We're some kind of cousins, just like everyone else in Brightwater. He used to quote a poem, by Horace, about everyone falling in love with the wrong person. A savage joke, he used to say. Those words really stuck in my mind. A savage joke."

"Saevo mittere cum ioco," I quoted softly.

"Those are the words. The very ones," he said. "You remind me a lot of your mother. Learned and pretty both."

"And what about you, Gus?" I asked, emboldened by the whiskey and the nostalgic first spring day, both of which fostered a strange intimacy. "Did you ever fall in love?"

He beamed and raised his glass. "Eh-uh. Many times. Can't tell you how many pretty ladies had my heart for a while. But the trouble was, I had given my heart already as just a boy. To the sea. And she's a jealous mistress. Yessir,, Athena. A jealous mistress." He mused for a minute, but suddenly his look grew more intense as he studied the water. "There's a storm coming. A bad one."

"A storm?" His elegiac tone had made me think for a minute that he was speaking in metaphors. "You mean a real one?"

His silent chuckle shook him again. "A real one. Don't let this clearing fool you, Athena. The clearing wind shouldn't box the compass. It ought to clear to the northwest then settle into the west and southwest. Nope. That storm's out there waiting to come back twice as bad for standing offshore getting back its strength. Line storms we call them, because they happen around the time the sun crosses the line."

"The equinox?"

"Eh-yuh. Friday maybe. Saturday for sure."

"I hope it doesn't spoil the dance."

Again the silent chuckle convulsed him. "Ought to provide a lot of fun for folks all dressed up, no place to go, in the Castle. Should be the best party of the year. Speaking of a party, Athena, can you stay for lunch? I'll be heating up some chowder for Jack from Point's End who's going to help me put over a mooring that won't drag in the line storm."

"Thanks, Gus," I said, "but I've already been invited for lunch at Bluecove. Maybe another time."

He stood up and took off his cap, and we shook hands cordially. I descended the porch steps and crossed the lawn toward the beach. At the opening in the stone wall I turned and waved, and Gus waved back. I saw a pickup truck with a large winch park in front of his house before I latched the gate behind me and picked my way down the flagstone steps set into the bluff until I reached the shore of the ocean.

It was half tide. The sand was swept clean of all but the droll footsteps of the birds. The blue of the sky melted into the deeper blue of the sea with the distant fog hanging like a curtain between. Along the bluff the bare wild rose and bayberry bushes bowed slightly under the breeze, and before me the rollers creamed along the shore, still strong but wearied by their journey from Spain. A seagull approached me inquisitively and, disappointed that I was empty handed, took off with a cry and wheeled inland. I thought of the Great Lakes seagull of the schoolyard only two days before. It seemed a world and a lifetime away, I thought, as I turned on my way back to the Castle and then on to Bluecove.

CHAPTER NINE

My room at the castle was filled with sunlight from the big window, and it was much easier to open the safe than it had been in the darkness of the previous night. I took the box of papers out of the safe and but it into my backpack.

My talk with Miss Adams had startled me into realizing that my reluctance to give the papers to Montero was largely based on suspicions planted by her own fears. Now it appeared that those fears were the product of a mind temporarily deranged by her illness.

Whether or not that illness was in fact caused by deliberate poisoning was a problem I could not solve. I seemed to have no choice but to hand over the provenance and get it over with.

Montero's invitation for lunch had been for 1:00 and it was not yet noon, but I thought that I would leave early so as to have time to explore the beach near Bluecove. I disciplined my hair, put on a clean turtleneck and my best embroidered cardigan and my boat moccasins, suitable for walking on the beach. For luck, I fastened around my neck the gold locket, inherited from my mother, which held tiny snapshots of both parents, taken on Crete when they were both young together.

I opened the window of my car as I crossed the causeway. On that scented April morning, all of Brightwater seemed to have taken to the streets, coats open to the sun. A restaurant had drawn back the canvas and plastic awning from its sidewalk cafe, and ladies with their winter coats thrown over the chair backs drank coffee and wine at little tables.

One side of College Hill slopes down to the canal and its two bridges, the Fenderbog Road and the highway to the mainland. Another drops first through the city and then the open fields of farms and old summer estates to the ocean shore, with the long stretch of Squanocket Point and Point's End extending out beyond the rocky headlands around the inlet of Bluecove. As the buildings of the city fell away behind me, I could look down the road and see the ocean.

Unfamiliar as I was with the main road, I drove until I saw a sign pointing to public parking for the beach. I turned off the road to a sand-dusted parking lot behind the dunes. I carried the box with me for safe keeping as I walked out on the beach, where I sat down on a sun-warmed rock. I looked from the lighthouse on one side down the sweep of white sand to the headlands of slate and quartz which surrounded Bluecove and then, beyond, up the distant hill to the gothic towers of the university. In the haze, the landscape seemed as lovely as a dream, remote as a vision.

Contemplating this remoteness, I felt as if the April sun were melting a heart frozen and numbed by the pain and losses of the winter, so that for the first time, except for that brief moment in Montero's arms in the driveway at Oakhill, I felt an upsurge of strong but conflicting emotions. I had lost both my only parent and his well-meant but oppressive domination. I was alone and vulnerable but also free and independent in a beautiful place. My new life seemed as mysterious and intriguing, as vast and potentially dangerous as the sea before me. I was only slowly becoming accustomed to my freedom, the freedom to live as I pleased. All I needed to do was to give the papers to Montero and enable him to complete the transaction with Bartholemew Badger.

And yet ... and yet. The doubts of the previous night came crowding back, even more coherent now that I had time alone to think things out and was not driven by frightened instinct. The Trapper family claimed ownership of the Athena, surely on reasonable grounds. *Would Emma simply relinquish her claim at our request?* It seemed unlikely. *What was the danger that my father and Ned spoke of so often? They both appeared to trust Montero completely. Did the danger lie with Jared...Or Emma? Then why did Montero appear to be so close to Emma and even, in spite of the friction between them, to Jared?*

Well, according to Gus's tale, which still had my head spinning, they were first cousins. Jared was the son of William Courtney, and Montero was the son of William's older brother, the late Judge Courtney. I didn't even want to try to sort out the tangled Fender family. Once again my sense of isolation began to oppress me. I found myself wishing, in defiance of the beauty of the ocean beach around me, that I had never left my comfortable and familiar life in Michigan.

"This is awful," I said aloud to myself. "I even miss Luis." Although the thought made me smile, I had to admit that it was true. For years I had been able to depend on a comfortable level of male companionship, an elbow next to mine on a theater seat, an arm along the back of the car seat, a chaste but warm embrace to end a Saturday night. Well, Luis was no longer available, and in an hour or so I would relinquish even the papers, the last link to my old life.

I looked up and saw a lone figure approaching from the direction of Bluecove. I knew him at once, the tall thin build, the quick stride, and the broad shoulders, one higher than the other. I slid down from the rock, and, as I hesitated, another figure of almost identical height and build appeared from behind the promontory. It was a young man of about twenty dressed in a sweater and jeans.

"There you are," said Montero. "I'm glad you're here. What do you think of my beach?"

I approached them along the damp sand below the high water line. "It's beautiful," I said. "It's nicer than Agios Titos."

"But Agios Titos is very nice," he responded with his quick smile." The seagulls soared and screamed above us.

"I'm afraid your birds aren't as tuneful as the nightingale," I said. "But I like them. They sound so free."

The young man looked from one of us to the other. "This is my son Victor. Victor, this is Athena Grey."

Victor gave me a hand. "How do you do, Miss Grey."

"Please call me Athena."

His gaze was fresh and frank and intelligent. With the bright waves of his hair, his long mouth and urbane charm, he seemed familiar, but I couldn't think whom he resembled. His face was like Montero's in the high forehead and prominent cheekbones, but his eyes were large and brown, and his skin, a warm peach tan, was darker than his gold hair. Then he smiled, and the dazzle of perfect white teeth was Emma's.

I felt as if a little cold hand gripped my heart and caused it to shrivel. The clear resemblance answered the question which had caused me such puzzlement just minutes before.

"I have never been to Crete," he said, "but I'd really like to go. If my Dad gets a grant next summer, he says he will take me. Will you be going, too?"

"I don't know," I said.

"Are you coming back to lunch at Bluecove?" Montero's voice was flat and formal, but Victor turned his eyes and smile on me.

"My Uncle Will is down from Cambridge for the week. I know he would like to see you. He talks a lot about the summer on Crete when you were little and knew more about archeology than most grownups."

"It would be a pleasure," I said.

"Victor, would you go back and tell Grandma that Athena is here and we'll be up in just a few minutes?" Montero said.

"Sure." Victor walked back along the beach at the high water mark. The seagulls flew up at his approach and dropped back behind him.

As soon as he was out of sight around the promontory that divided the ocean beach from the cove, Montero extended his hand to touch the box that I carried balanced on one hip. "Is that — are those — the provenance?"

"Yes."

"My God. I can't believe it. After all these years. If only Robert. And Sophie. My dear..." He broke off, unable to continue. I handed the box from my two hands into his.

"Thank you," he said.

"I'm afraid."

"I wish I could say that you were wrong, but it is only wise to be afraid. Trust me, Athena. We will see this thing through to the end."

He turned, and I followed him around the rocky promontory to the shore of the cove. There was a sudden stillness here, for the rocks cut off the southwest wind, and the cove was sheltered from the ocean surf. The wall of slate and quartz rose behind us, but here in the middle of the cove, the land sloped down to a little valley through which a fresh water stream emptied into the sea. Some distance inland, the stream was spanned by the arch of an old railway bridge. To the right of that, the bluff was crowned by a stone wall and green lawn, beyond which the house was visible, white and mellow among the wind-stunted maple trees.

"What a beautiful spot this is," I said.

"Yes. I love it. And it has been good for Victor to grow up in such a place."

We were walking toward the spot near the stream from which stepping stones of slate mounted the bluff to the lawn. After a while he stopped, blocking my way. "You will be staying, won't you?"

"Staying? Here?"

"At the Castle. We need you. The new contracts usually come out in mid-April. Would you be willing to stay on for a year at least? Or preferably three years?"

"I... I don't know. I'll need some time to think about it. "

"Are you unhappy here?"

"I really don't know," I repeated. "It's just... it seems as if I have suddenly realized how much I have lost, in such a short time. My father, of course, but also my whole life. My only home. My students I thought, after I met you again, after I came here, everything would be all right. But, somehow, it's not."

He turned back toward the house. "No," he said. "It's not." We resumed our climb up the bluff, he still carrying the box. "But not because of you, Athena. You must understand that. Could I ask you to stay through this year? It's terribly important to me. You will understand in just a few days. You could finish your thesis here. We would be happy to send you back to Ann Arbor to talk to your advisor whenever you needed to. I've known him since he was Will's section man."

"Thank you," I repeated. A lump formed in my throat. My freshly thawed heart was melting rapidly under his kindness. I turned my head so that he wouldn't see the tears in my eyes, and we walked together across the flagstone terrace to the back door of the house. There seemed to be a tension between us, as if our adjacent arms were joined by trilling wires. I could feel his nearness on my skin.

A book-lined study opened to the left of the back door. This was in fact the room that I had pictured around him when first we met, although a little more faded and dusty and piled with books and papers everywhere. In the corner by the fireplace, a tall man in his sixties sat in a wing chair writing in a notebook balanced on his knee. He stood, and the grey cat which had lain on his shoulders re-established itself on the back of the chair. He leaned on a cane as he crossed the room. The brace on his right foot supported the injury suffered during his captivity. Although his hair was white above a long, lined face, he had the same black-lashed Irish eyes as his nephew; and the smile that I knew so well flashed from the corners of his mouth to the corners of his eyes. It was the chief excavator of Agios Titos, my father's mentor, William Courtney.

"Athena, my dear. Welcome to Bluecove." I remembered the terrace at Agios Titos and the sound of the cicadas and nightingales and the scent of oranges as the grown-ups talked and laughed. He bent, and his mustache brushed my cheek as he kissed me.

"You haven't changed at all," I said.

"Ah, but you have," he smiled. And how we have waited for you. Are these the papers?"

Montero laid the box on the writing table, and both men stood bending over me as I drew my car keys out of my jacket pocket and opened the little lock. William's hands trembled as he carefully lifted out the documents and began to sort them into groups. They both sat down and began to pore over them in silence.

"Here," William said at length, noticing that I was still standing. He drew me down to the chair beside him. "Sit here, Athena. This concerns you more than anyone." Presently he added, "Can you construe this? Both my eyes and my Byzantine Greek are failing." I helped him with a translation, and soon I was as absorbed in the task as my companions.

"Robert's will?" Montero asked at length. "And the letter from Bart Badger?"

"They're in my room at the Castle," I said. "In the safe."

After a long silence, both men finished reading and looked up at the same time, their eyes meeting in a moment of shared exultation.

"My God!" Montero repeated.

"It's all here," William said. "You can go ahead with your plan. Except for Emma. I will not..."

Montero cleared his throat, a sudden warning sound, as lacking in subtlety as a kick in the ankle.

William gave him a quick interrogatory glance, and Montero responded with an almost imperceptible raising of his chin. But I understood that gesture. It was the Greek signal for "oxi" or `no'. Even here, in the affectionate presence of this kindly man, I was once again made to feel like an outsider.

"What plan?" I asked. Again their glances interlocked. Neither answered. "You can't leave me out of it." I was growing angry. "It concerns me more than either of you."

"You're right," William said. "She's not a child, Monty."

"I won't put you in a dangerous situation..."

I sprang to my feet, furious at his domineering which now as before struck me as patronizing and arrogant.

"Monty, dear." A voice like a tenor bell rang from the doorway, and I drew breath, unclenched my fists, and turned, masking my rage with a polite smile. Although the short hair that sprang from her high forehead was now white, I recognized Maude Montero at once from old pictures of her in the role of Shaw's *St.*

Joan. She was over six feet tall, with large, clear brown eyes, and she carried herself with the grace of a much younger woman. "And you must be Athena. Lunch is ready. Will you join us?" She took my hand and led me through the door.

"We'll be there in just two minutes, Maudie," William said. "We need to pack these papers up."

The door closed behind us but then sprang open under the breeze from the back door. I heard William's voice, startlingly harsh. "Don't be a fool. You'll ruin your life, just as mine was ruined."

"That's for me to choose," Montero said, and his voice was also hard.

"And it's no favor to her."

"You know she's wanted it for years."

"Nonsense..." the door swung shut again.

Although it had the traits of the family dining room of novels and plays, an antique table with mismatched chairs, a sideboard laden with tarnished Victorian silver, family portraits and faded landscapes on the walls; there was a homely eccentricity about the room. The upright piano held piles of music, a flute and a violin as well as a pair of sneakers and an assemblage of snapshots. The centerpiece was a spray of forsythia in a mason jar. Victor was already standing at his place, and he pulled out the chair beside him for me. Montero carved the chicken and handed my plate down to his mother, who added asparagus and roasted potatoes.

"Would you like a crazy salad with your meat?" asked Victor passing me the glass bowl. *A teen-ager who quotes Yeats,* I thought, *will be an easy friend to have.*

"Thank you," I said. "I'm flattered."

"Well, you must be a fine woman," Victor said in a confidential tone, "because Dad is so happy you came here to work. He came home that day a changed man."

But he had been overheard. "Shut up, Victor," said Montero, but he was laughing along with the others.

"There I go again, another gaffe," Victor murmured, this time safe beneath the general commotion. "You should have seen them the time I asked why Dad looked so much like Jared."

Whether William, across from us, had heard or not I couldn't tell, but he rescued the conversation, pouring wine out of an ancient decanter with no stopper. "What is your thesis about, Athena?"

"The earliest cult of Athena in the Aegean period. I guess she fascinates me, like a patron saint."

"Do you know the Agios Titos Athena? The real one, I mean? The prehistoric one?"

"Only from photographs. I don't remember seeing it when I was little. But the Brightwater Athena is also real, you know."

Faces froze. Silver clicked on plates. "What is going on here?" my mind asked in a panic. The papers, the provenance proving her authenticity, were right in the next room, but apparently we didn't mention that. I felt like poor Victor, committing gaffes, and I don't even know these giant beautiful people. Yet they were supposed to be my oldest friends in the world.

"I remember your parents so well," said Mrs. Courtney at length, and Montero and William breathed out and began to eat again. "They spent several years here when they were graduate students at the university. They often came to dinner here when Luke was still alive." Her eyes flickered to a photograph on the mantel, an older, broader version of William, with the same Irish eyes and long Yankee face. "We were second cousins. Amelia Courtney married Juan Montero, a wine merchant from Spain who came to Brightwater with a shipment of sherry and never went home after he met Amelia." The Courtney smile flashed across her face and then around the table. "Amelia's mother was a Howe, whose mother was also a Courtney. We're all related, it seems." The thought occurred to me that she might have overheard Victor's confidence.

"Maudie, I thought it was only southern women who explained their entire genealogy to new friends," said William.

"I think it is an east coast phenomenon," said Montero. "It can be traced from Halifax to Savannah along the route of the three masted schooners. More chicken, Victor?"

"Thanks, Dad."

"When you're finished, I'll give you a lift back to the college. Athena, could we drive you?"

"No thanks. I'm parked at the public beach."

"Will you be at your desk later? I'll finally tell you about the section — not that you couldn't do it on your own. But I've been neglecting my new assistant outrageously."

"Four o'clock?"

"Perfect. We can go from there to Emmy's for supper. More chicken?"

"No, thanks. This is a wonderful lunch," I added as William refilled my wineglass.

"It's really dinner," Mrs. Courtney explained. "We dine at noon because I have to be at the Brightwater Theater early."

"What are you doing now?" I asked.

"I am rehearsing *Lady Macbeth* and doing Queen Gertrude, a marvelous role, with a sort of Byronic anguish over the loss of innocence — that finally irreparable loss."

William, leaning back and caressing his wineglass with one long hand, quoted, "But if the while I think on thee, dear friend— All losses are restored and sorrows end." Unexpectedly, his eyes misted, and he reached across the table and laid his hand on mine. "I was sorry to hear of your father, my dear. I was fond of him."

His emotion was contagious. My own tears, helped perhaps by Gus's whiskey and the Courtney wine, as well as my sense of loss over my father's papers and the tension of our meeting in the study, were again close to the surface. Reminded all the more keenly by this comfortable family atmosphere of my own status as an outsider, I was afraid that if I began to weep I would never stop. "Thank you," I managed and, turning in panic to the matriarch, I added, "Let me help you wash up."

"And I as well," said William, heaving himself to his feet.

"I won't hear of it. The dessert is on the sideboard. Help yourselves, and then go and enjoy the rest of your vacation. You know you have to be back in Cambridge on Monday. Athena and I shall manage perfectly." I carried dishes through the swinging door as if I, not they, were made of china. Once safely in the kitchen, I sat at the table and buried my face in my hands until I felt a brisk pat on my shoulder.

"Now then," said Mrs. Courtney. "Brandy or coffee, or both?"

"Coffee, please," I managed, breathing deeply. "I'm afraid the wine is what set me off. On top of the whiskey I had with Gus."

"Cousin Gus? Squire Howe? Isn't he a delight? Four fingers of whiskey in a jelly glass at ten in the morning?"

"Eleven."

"Probably wanted to make a good first impression." She poured two cups of coffee and sat across from me. I drank deeply and began to recover myself. "Better now?"

The phrase, apparently a family byword, brought back the comforting gesture of the night before and then inexorably the realization that there was more than one cause for my grief.

"Yes. I think so. I'm afraid it's because I didn't cry at the time, except just once."

"One can never cry enough at the time," old Maude said. "Loss is loss. It can't be helped. There isn't any remedy. You just learn to bear it." She looked over the windowsill clutter of potted herbs and sprouting avocado seeds to the driveway where William was sending off Montero and Victor in the jeep. "I wish I could convince these men of that. My poor Courtney's. Will pining away for one woman for nearly forty years. And Monty." She turned her dark eyes to me. "Did you know about the boy?"

"He... he told me about him in Michigan, in the winter."

"Did he tell you who the mother was?"

"No."

"Always the gentleman. Can you guess?"

"Yes."

"Poor Emma. She was only fifteen at the time. It was the year her poor mother finally drank and doped herself to death, leaving Emma in the gardener's cottage with a hired nanny. She came to us here and said that she was pregnant with Monty's child. He was in Greece at the time, which of course, made the fact impossible. It had to be our illustrious cousin Jared, who had gotten himself into other trouble. My dear Luke had had him sent off to a very good boarding school in the mid-west." She rose and stood looking out the window.

"Poor Emma. Why should she try to deceive us? We would have taken her in. We were all she had. You must remember how young they all were. The boys were sixteen. Brightwater is a small town during the off season. Once the summer people go home, we natives don't have much to do except talk about each other. And Emma has always been weak. All she had were her looks; her best hope was a good marriage. We were more her family than her poor mother had ever been. We took her in, of course, drove her to Boston to see her doctor. The amazing thing is that nobody in Brightwater seems to have learned that she was pregnant. Monty came home just before Victor was born at the Boston Lying-In, a scrawny little thing, only six pounds. Emma recovered quickly, and Luke and I sent her off to boarding school in New Hampshire. Monty had gotten attached to the little fellow, so we kept him here. He almost didn't live until his first birthday — terrible food allergies. Monty often held him all night, not knowing if he would see the morning. Of course, Luke and Will and I took our turns. Then after his first year he began to thrive and made up for lost time. We loved him. Still do, of course. Emma soon released him, and Monty adopted him, although there was no need. There have always been stray lambs at Bluecove."

She sighed and drained her coffee cup. "That's our problem now. We seem to be nothing but stray lambs. Me a widow, poor Will still carrying a torch for Veronica Fender, and Monty a grown man living with his mother. It's not natural. I would like to move into town, closer to the theater, where I can make myself a new life, not looking to see Luke again wherever I turn. I would like to see Monty settled here as the head of Bluecove. But I will not leave my place to poor Emma." Her face, with its hollow cheeks and temple, its marks of age, its stern beauty, was like that of some ancient Sybil.

"Why are you telling this to me, a stranger?" I asked.

"I don't know. Except that you're not really a stranger. He was just a boy when he went off to that first expedition to Crete. Robert and Sophie were almost like surrogate parents for the summer. But, faced with Victor on his return, he had to grow up overnight. But Victor, much as he loves his home, is starting his own life. It seems as if Monty is at a crucial point..." she left the sentence unfinished.

I stood up. With that sudden smile, she drew a handkerchief from her pocket and wiped my face. "There. Pretty thing that you are, don't listen to me. You have your own worries."

"I — I must go now," I said, and, even forgetting to thank her for lunch, I let myself out the back door.

A damp chill had fallen over the afternoon. The tide had ebbed, and the clam flats smelled of seaweed and dead fish. Around the headland, the ocean wind drove through my clothes, and I shivered as I walked to my car.

CHAPTER TEN

It was indeed the setting I had pictured for him, I thought as I drove back to the city: a house filled with firelight and books and family history, old silver and polished tables and worn Persian rugs. Even their light, rapid New England speech, which sounded almost British to me, increased my sense of isolation. His whole life, his very genetic makeup, was deeply woven into the warp and woof of this little man-made island on which I was a stranger. It was hard enough that, having just handed over to him my only legacy from my father, I felt wholly bereft. I was an outsider, an interloper in a strange place.

There is a universal cure for such a malaise. I needed a new dress for the dance. Jared was, after all, an attractive man; and, like me, he seemed something of an outsider, a bystander who watched his fellow mortals from behind the blank inscrutability of that dark and handsome face.

At the top of College Hill, parallel to Market Street, ran Pleasant Avenue, one of the most fashionable shopping streets in New England. Although some of the shops were closed until the summer people came back, most of them were open. Clutching the purse that contained my pay from Ann Arbor, I sank ankle deep into the apricot carpeting of a dress shop and waited until a saleslady in rustling black asked to help me.

"I need an evening dress for the museum ball," I said. "Size four or six petite. Perhaps red."

She gave me the analytical look of a painter appraising a model, and her eyes widened briefly. "This way, please, Miss. I have the very thing." She led me to a dressing room bigger than my kitchen and left me alone with my shabby reflection in a three-way mirror. Soon she returned with a froth of red chiffon over one arm. She threw it on over my greyish slip, fastened up the back, and stepped back with the air of a magician.

The effect was remarkable. Even I, who never look pretty to myself, gasped with pleasure. The red warmed my coloring. The cut made a Dresden shepherdess of my gymnast's figure. As I turned and posed, the saleswoman left and returned with a pair of shoes which would cost me as much as a week's meals. Back at the cash register, I completed the afternoon's folly by buying underwear of scandalous cut, red and lavishly trimmed with lace. *Retail therapy indeed.*

Back at the Castle, I had to hurry to put away my new finery before meeting Montero at my desk at four. He was grave and rather subdued when he arrived, and we walked up the hill to the college together in silence. He showed me my classroom in a collegiate gothic building. It was the old fashioned kind, with a platform for the desk and ivy insinuating itself though the casement windows. After taking me around to meet the other members of the department, he took me into the room where slides were stored in walls of drawers. He turned on the light under the glass slide table and drew out a chair for me before sitting down beside me.

"I'm working on tomorrow's all university lecture," he said, "which you'll be discussing with the section on Friday." His face, lighted by an odd radiance from the slide table, was intent as he arranged a number of slides. "I'm not sure whether to do the metopes or the ionic frieze first. What do you think?"

"There seems to be a natural sequence from the cruder metopes to the better ones and then to the frieze and finally to the pediment sculptures." I demonstrated the sequence as I spoke, ending with the river god, surely one of the most seductive works of art ever made.

"Of course. Do you think I should include any other models of the Athena Parthenos besides ours?"

"I'd say no. The little bronze in Athens is so ugly. In fact, ours is the only one that can stand up to the Elgin marbles."

"You're right."

We worked together in quiet professional harmony until we had finished the sequence for both his lecture and the classes for the following week. At length he pushed his chair back from the slide table and stretched, easing his neck. "It's so good to have you here," he said. "I missed you this winter. There were several times I almost called you, just to see how you were. At least now I can keep an eye on you."

Did he ever think, as I did so often, of our parting in the driveway at Oakhill? "You promised to tell me the plan," I said.

He stood up abruptly and began to pace. "It's something that Robert and Will and I began twenty years ago, as a result of the Agios Titos expedition. And Sophie, of course. She was still alive. We had come to realize that the monument had to be hers, but the documentary evidence was incomplete. So Robert started working on it, first for her sake and then for yours. Finishing it as he did just before he died was the first step. Then we, the three of us, had to find a way to get actual possession of the Athena."

"And did you? Find one, I mean?"

"Yes. That, I think, will be surprisingly easy. And we'll be getting help from Badger."

"But what about Emma Trapper?"

He turned his back to me and stood looking out the window. "What do you mean?"

"You know what I mean. She thinks it is hers."

"I have solved that problem, too, I think, although... Will disagrees. But it can't be helped."

"You sound depressed."

"Do I?" He kept his back to me. "You are much too perceptive."

"Only about you."

Then ensuing silence was broken by the pealing of the university carillon announcing five o'clock. He wheeled around, glaring at his watch. "Damn! I promised Emmy I would help with dinner. We must fly. Do you know where the cottage is? Shall I call for you?" He disposed of slides, tightened his tie, and shrugged into his jacket.

"No, thanks. Jared said that he would meet me at six."

"Jared," said Montero. "Yes. Well. Is that all you're wearing? Bring something warm for the evening. The fog here can be chilly." He guided me to the door and locked it behind us. He was once again silent descending the hill and preoccupied as he politely took his leave at the castle door.

I dressed with great care in my prettiest dress from Ann Arbor, and when Jared called for me at my door, I was awarded with a quick flare of appreciation in his eyes before his face resumed its normal deadpan. He guided my hand to the crook of his elbow as we descended one of the great staircases. "Have you had the tour of Howe's Island?" he asked.

"I dropped in to visit Gus Howe this morning," I said, "so I've seen his house."

"One of the oldest on the Point, about 1680, although there have been renovations since then. The Howe's used to own this island and a good part of the Point until old Freddy Trapper ruined Gus's father. They were among the original settlers of the Point. In fact, the first two were Elizabeth Howe, a protestant visionary, and Lord Peter Fender, the younger son of a royalist duke. The Point made a good refuge for both cavaliers and Puritans in those days."

"Any relation?"

"Of course. One of the few New England families to bear arms." He opened the great door and we stepped out into the westering sun. "But we Fenders have long since fallen on hard times."

We walked around the side of the Castle to a terrace in the back, from which a flight of steps descended to a garden worthy of a Roman villa. The wind had dropped, and the day's sun had melted most of the ice and snow. Here and there in the borders green shoots of daffodils emerged from the damp ground. We strolled arm in arm down a path between leafless hedges from which the chickadees peered at us brightly. In the center of a fishpond, an ornamental fountain stood silent and overgrown with weeds. A bare rose arbor led to an orchard beyond, where the newly-thawed turf sank beneath our feet. Beyond that there was a kitchen garden, empty now except for a few shoots of asparagus against the south side of a stone wall and the low-growing thyme which scented the air as we walked on it. Jared opened a gate in the stone wall and stood back to let me through. The path led to a slate-roofed cottage, studiedly quaint, with bow windows and miniature turrets mimicking those of the Castle. I saw that Montero's jeep was parked at the side, next to a vintage Jaguar convertible.

The front hall was empty except for a carved staircase, again a quotation of the architecture of the Castle. The living room to the left was furnished only with a grand piano, the built-in window seats, and a long table, splendid with white damask and silver candelabra. Emma came forward, elegant in an African caftan and gold sandals. She pressed a scented cheek to each of ours and kissed the air in a festive cloud of champagne fumes.

"Do take a window seat. There's going to be a marvelous sunset in a minute. Monty's here opening the wine." As she spoke, he came through the swinging door from the kitchen carrying a tray with glasses and a bottle of champagne. "Cheers everyone," said Emma, raising her glass. "You came at a good time, Athena. We're finishing the last of Grandpapa's cellar. Dear Grandpapa." She slurred a little. "What would we have done without him?"

"Somewhat past its prime," Jared the connoisseur pronounced, "but still exquisite, like a great beauty in her old age." We touched glasses all around.

"Come to the window," Emma said. "We're about to have one of our famous Howe's Island sunsets." She lurched slightly, and Montero steadied her with a hand under her elbow.

The light filling the room went from gold to pink and a rich red before fading to lavender and then grey-rose. In silence, we watched the sun setting across the harbor, laying a gold track along the water, until the brightness faded from the sea and the radiance from the clouds, and the evening star hung in the opalescence like a little lamp. Montero switched on the light next to the piano, and the twilight became night.

In the distance I heard an unearthly wail, and, closer, a deep-voiced horn. "What's that?" I said. "The foghorn," said Jared. "The fog is coming in."

"It's late this evening," said Montero.

"Luckily," said Emma. "Perhaps it held off so that Athena could see the sunset."

Again I heard the strange wail.

"That's the Squanocket Point Light foghorn," Montero said to me. "And the deeper one is Courtney's reef, just south of here."

Emma laid the back of her hand to her brow. "My God, the fog! Sometimes I simply cannot bear it."

"I like it," said Montero. "Especially on the Point here. Makes me feel safe from the mainland."

"But that's just the trouble," Emma continued. "We're so isolated, so cooped up together, half drowned by the sea, half smothered by the fog."

"It's not the sea and the fog," said Jared. "It's the past." He rose and refilled all the glasses with champagne before he moved to the piano where a song book stood open on the rack. "Speaking of cooped up together," he said, "I remember these songs." His fingers coaxed some chords from the keys. "God, Emma. You haven't had this piano tuned since then. I'll come and do it myself one of these days."

"Do play anyway, Jared Darling, while Monty and I dish up." She stood a little unsteadily, and again Montero kept a hand under her arm as they went into the kitchen. Jared sat on the piano bench and played a few arpeggios, stopping occasionally to change a note to compensate for the piano's lack of tuning.

"Come sit beside me, little Athena," he said. "Do you sing? I usually put up with Emma's untuned piano because of the wonderful scores she inherited from old Freddy. Lovely things. She wanted me to sell them, but I refused, selfishly I'm afraid. But, as I explained to her, they will only increase in value." He was playing softly, the simple and haunting folk tunes on the rack before us as he spoke. "But tonight I'm in the mood for the good old songs." He turned the page, began a new song, and in a light baritone, sang the words.

> *Last night she slept on a goose feather bed*
> *Last night she slept with her new-wedded lord;*
> *But tonight she sleeps on the cold cold ground,*
> *And she sleeps with the black jack gypsy O,*
> *She sleeps with the black jack gypsy O.*

"Come join me. I need a soprano for the next verse."

"I can't sing without some more champagne," I said.

"Nor I. Would you pour?"

I refilled our glasses and joined him, at first shyly but with growing assurance as he leaned close enough to me to keep my voice on key.

Oh, what care I for my goose feather bed?
Oh what care I for my new-wedded lord?
For tonight I sleep on the cold cold ground,
But I sleep with the black jack gypsy O
I sleep with the black jack gypsy O.

Behind us, Montero and Emma moved around the table, lighting candles and pouring wine. Their voices joined us like a ghost chorus in the next ballad.

Down in the valley,
The valley so low,
Hang your head over,
Hear the wind blow.

Montero turned off the lamp, and the light from the fire and the candles filled the room with flickering warmth. Their voices drew nearer as they came up behind us.

Roses love sunshine.
Violets love dew,
Angels in heaven
Know I love you.

The others had begun to harmonize, leaving the melody to my thin soprano.

If you don't love me,
Love who you please,
Put your arms round me
Give my heart ease.

The piano continued softly after our voices were hushed, but then it too fell silent until Emma announced dinner.

Jared led me to the table where we all sat down to bowls of mussels in a broth of wine and herbs. "These are lovely," I said, grateful that my companions were attacking the shells as greedily as I. "Where do you buy them?"

Emma giggled. "My dear, they grow everywhere at low tide. You don't even have to dig them, just pull them off the rocks. They're best when they're little like this, although they're a nuisance to clean. But Monty doesn't mind, do you, darling?" She refilled her glass from the freshly opened bottle, dripping ice water on the tablecloth, and then aimed for my glass. Montero gracefully took the bottle from her hand, poured it around, and replaced it in the ice bucket. I wiped my hands on the damask napkin, a yard square but raveled at the edges.

"You'll have to show me where to find them," I said. I lowered my spoon into the wreckage of the shells to find the last of the beautiful broth. Montero stood and took my plate. "May I help?" I asked.

"Oh no," said Emma. "I can't bear to have anyone else in the kitchen. Except Monty, of course."

I accidentally kicked the table leg, and, looking down, saw that it was the leg of a sawhorse. Montero brought in a platter of pheasant and asparagus. We finished with a salad and cheese. Emma had talked vivaciously, as we all had, throughout the meal, but as the champagne supply dwindled, she grew silent and stared at the guttering flames of the candles.

"What a perfect evening," I said at last. "Starting with the sunset."

"You can see why we don't bother with television," Montero said.

"Who are you trying to kid?" Emma demanded suddenly. "She's not stupid." The slurring had grown pronounced. "She can see that I could never afford television, or even a decent meal, or a magazine to read. I've sold all the furniture. I live off the land. I didn't fool you for a minute, did I?"

I wanted to protest that, child of genteel academic poverty that I was, I had considered her hospitality as luxurious as it was generous; but before I could answer Montero said, "Athena's got to get back to the Castle now, Emmy. Thanks for a perfect meal. Now you deserve a nice rest."

Jared had risen, and he offered me his arm. "I'll take you back."

"Did you bring a coat?" Montero asked me sternly.

"No. It was so warm when we left."

"I left my car here earlier today," Jared said. "I'll drive you the little distance so you won't get chilled." Polite farewells were exchanged, and Jared propelled me out the front door. "Poor Emma," he said as he helped me into the Jaguar. "I guess you know that old Freddy's business was ruined by the crash of 1929, and of course, the rum running business went with Repeal. He gave the Castle to the college for taxes. Emma was left with the gardener's cottage. I think her whole salary goes to her preposterous wardrobe. If we her friends didn't feed her, she wouldn't eat." He got in beside me and started the engine.

"Does she have problems with her nerves?" I asked politely.

"Pills and booze." He answered shortly, driving slowly into the wall of fog. "Expensive habits, especially now that old Alfred's cellar is almost gone."

At the Castle he turned off the engine and the headlights. I shivered in the damp and reached for the door handle, but he held me back with an arm around my shoulders. "Here. I promised not to let you get chilled." For a moment I relaxed against his warmth, and he bent his head to mine. He kissed my temple and then my cheek. I had thought his mouth would be hard, but it was soft and warm, and his skin had a clean male scent mixed pleasantly with shaving soap and champagne.

"Please," I managed. "Jared. I hardly know you..."

"But I know you, my sweet Athena," he said, low. "I know your bright, ironic mind, old for your age from all those years alone with your father. I know your untamed heart. And your loneliness. Be still. Stay with me here, just for a moment." I heard the distant wail of the foghorn over his breathing. "I love you, Athena. I meant that song for you. You don't have to love me. It's enough that you want me."

Suddenly over his dark head I saw the door of the Castle open, sending a beam of light into the fog and framing the silhouette of Gus, who shone a flashlight over the parking lot. We sprang apart. Gus and his light were descending the stairs. "Good night, Jared," I said, a little winded.

"Good night, my sweet. Until tomorrow." He caught my hand and kissed it as I let myself out of the car, and Gus materialized beside me in the fog.

"There you are," he said. "Monty called. Wanted me to make sure you were safe home. Good night, Jared. Drive carefully in this. Give my respects to your folks." Jared did not respond, and his Jaguar purred away across the causeway.

I was grateful for the darkness, and I mounted the steps resentfully, feeling like a teen-ager caught necking on the porch.

Gus, however, remained his debonair self. "Don't be mortified, Athena." He said cheerfully. "Jared goes after all the prettiest girls. You should be flattered."

I burst out laughing, almost hysterical, but greatly relieved by his tact, and I was still giggling when he left me at my door. My heart was still pounding, however, and even a long shower, worthy of Lady Macbeth failed to calm me down. The entire day had overstimulated me, and I pondered the fact that here in Puritan New England I had experienced in twelve hours, more drinking, socializing and lovemaking than I had ever undertaken in so short a time in Michigan. I had to read one of Miss Adams' paperbacks far into the night before sleep finally came.

CHAPTER ELEVEN

The last slide of Thursday's lecture was the facade of the Parthenon, springing as if alive between modern Athens and the Greek sky. Montero had finished speaking, but a silence still lay over the darkened hall. Then the slide went off and the lights went on and the storm of applause continued until people began to leave their seats for the reception in the foyer outside the auditorium.

"I want to go right to the British Museum and steal them back," said the woman undergraduate next to me. "Isn't he great?"

"He really is," I said. I was familiar with the account of Lord Elgin's raid on the Acropolis and the futile attempts of the Greek government to recover its own national treasure — it had been important to my father but I had still found Montero's account profoundly moving.

"Aren't you just in love with him?" the student said, standing and shouldering her backpack. "Like, I said to my boyfriend last week, I go, 'too bad you don't look more like Professor Courtney because all us girls have a crush on him.' And he goes, 'Just give me time because he must be forty at least." She laughed and edged out of the row of seats. "See you around. Take it easy."

I had not heard his approach, so I was startled when his hand rested on my shoulder. I looked up. "It means a lot to you," he said.

"Yes. Of course. My upbringing."

He stepped over my knees and perched on the seat next to me. "Athena," he said, "I am going to be needing your help on Saturday night. It's terribly important, and it might even be dangerous."

"Professor Courtney. Oh. Excuse me." It was the rich voice of the college president, a silver haired man in a Brooks Brothers suit. Montero started up, and this time I, too, stood to let him past me into the aisle. Another man stepped out from behind the president, and I recognized the governor of the state. "Governor, you have met Professor Courtney, and err."

"My assistant. Miss Grey."

Polite greetings were exchanged. The president put an arm around Montero's shoulder. "The governor wanted to talk to you about this humanities grant." The three men walked toward the reception in the hall, where the sound of conversation was reaching a crescendo around the punch bowls. I followed until I paused in the doorway.

At the nearest table, Jared was standing with his hands resting on the handles of a wheelchair in which was sitting a man of striking appearance. He was of massive build, but more strong than fat, with chest and shoulders overdeveloped in compensation for his shrunken legs. His head was thrown back so that his mane of silver hair lay along his collar, and his regular features would have been handsome except that his stillness and pallor, for his face was as colorless as his hair, made him appear so corpse-like that I felt a chill at the sight of him and was almost surprised to notice that he was moving one hand on the arm of his wheelchair.

He was watching William and Maude Courtney, who were conversing with the woman who stood beside him, slim and dark with brilliant eyes and one white streak through the long hair swept back to a chignon at the nape of her neck. She was as straight and radiant as a candle flame. She must be Veronica Fender, the handsomest woman in Brightwater, as Gus had described her. As I stared, Jared looked up, and his eyes met mine. I stepped back behind the doorframe and leaned my back against the wall.

I was afraid of Jared Fender. I was afraid of my attraction to him, but most of all I was terrified by the aura of hatred, more powerful than any love, which bound him to the corpselike man in the wheelchair. *But he isn't dead. He is alive. Why did I think that?* I took deep breaths until I stopped trembling and ventured into the doorway again.

Of course he was alive. He spoke and elicited laughter from the circle around him, which had expanded to include Montero, the president and governor and now Emma, dazzling in azure silk. Once again I felt the sense of alienation, of exclusion from a closed circle, which had oppressed me since I first came to Brightwater. I stepped back from the doorway again and soon found my way up the back stairs to my rooms, where I lit a fire in the fireplace and brewed a cup of tea in the kitchen. I sat on the window seat, letting the coziness of the room comfort me.

There was still a muffled roar from the party beneath me. From the Squanocket Point Lighthouse, the foghorn spoke out to sea its warning of danger and was answered from Courtney's Reef. I stood up and began to pace, too restless even to settle down to Miss Adams' scary novel. I studied my bookshelves, looking for a text difficult enough to engage and distract my mind, and found my father's copy of *Horace*, worn and frayed from the touch of his hands. Remembering with a smile my conversation with Gus, I opened it to the ode he had quoted.

> *Quam turpi Pholoe peccat adultero*
> *Sic visum Veneri, cui placet imparis*
> *Formas atque animos sub iuga aenea*
> *Saeve mittere cum ioco.*

"Lycoris loves Cyrus, and Cyrus turns to cruel Pholoe, who would rather mate with wolves than sin with such a lecher. This is seen to by Venus, who is pleased to place unsuited minds and bodies beneath her brazen yoke, with a savage joke," I translated aloud. I thought of the many times in high school and college that my father had helped me with my *Horace*, and we had smiled together over the poet's gentle, worldly-wise irony.

I took the book back to the window seat and soon lost myself in a nostalgic return to the pleasures of sharing a bottle of old Falernian with Maecenas beneath the trees of the Sabine farm until it seemed that I was once again safe in an innocent time beneath my father's roof, far from the wail of the foghorn and the sinister people of Brightwater.

I awoke later with a start, slumped on the window seat, cold and stiff and certain that I had been awakened by a sound.

A human sound.

I listened again but heard nothing except the dialogue of the foghorns. I turned off my light and saw a faint light shining through the crack beneath my door. I slipped off my shoes and let myself out my door, carefully holding the latch so that it made no sound as it closed.

The door of the bedroom down the hall was ajar, and a light shone from it out into the hall. I crept along the wall until I could see into the room. Almost immediately I started back, retreating to my room as soundlessly as I had left it, locking the door and leaning against it, closing my eyes as if to efface the scene that seemed to have printed itself on the inside of my eyelids. But it would not go away. I saw the dimly lighted chamber with its canopied bed, the curtains drawn back to reveal the two figures lying asleep. The sheet covered the man to his waist, but his back was bare, and I knew that back. I had felt its smooth planes beneath his shirt the night before. It was Jared, and his dark hair was tousled and mingled with the long golden hair of Emma as she lay in his arms, in the total rest of long familiarity.

A savage joke indeed.

Well, back to the copy of *Horace*, which still lay face down on the window seat, and a long struggle with the interlocking gears of his language, so different from the lucid flow of Greek, before I was tired enough to go to bed.

When Jared appeared at my desk the next morning, I kept busy for a minute fumbling with my computer until I was composed.

"I missed you last night," he said. "I had hoped that you would meet my family."

"I had a lot to do."

"Are you angry at me, little Athena? It was my fault. I took unforgiveable liberties." I felt my color rising.

"Not at all," I said.

"I must talk to you. It is terribly important." Where had I heard that before?

"Jared. I have to leave. I have to meet Montero. I'm teaching my first section this morning. I need his help."

There was a flare of anger in his eyes, and the muscles of his jaw rippled. "How trusting you are. But you are so innocent. How can you have anything to do with that...with a man whose publication destroyed your father's life's work. And now he is plotting to steal the monument he discredited. Yes. You know it, don't you, although you try to deny the truth. He is scheming to steal the only inheritance, the only wealth of a woman who has lived in poverty all her life. Emma's father left her the Brightwater Athena. It is hers and nobody else's."

"Why are you saying this to me?" But I knew the answer before he spoke again.

"If you can give Emma your father's papers, the provenance of the Athena, then Courtney's scheme of robbery is foiled. It is easy to fence a pretty bauble for money, but not one of the major monuments of the world." He took my hand, and I was so relieved that he was ignorant of Montero's possession of the papers that I didn't object. The doorbell announcing the arrival of the Brightwater Pops Orchestra rescued me.

"A Mrs. Trapper said it was all right to rehearse here this morning, right?" said the young conductor. Emma had telephoned me earlier to say that she would not be in that morning because of a sick headache.

"Yes. Yes. Of course."

"She said the ball room."

"This way." I led him and his followers up one of the double staircases.

"Like wow," said the double bass, looking around.

"If you need anything and I'm not at my desk, just call Mr. Howe." I gave him the number. "If he isn't there, one of his staff will be."

"Thank you, Miss..."

"Grey. Athena Grey."

"Athena. Here, in Brightwater. I love it." We shook hands, beaming. The musicians began opening their cases and setting up their music stands. I heard Jared's step outside the ballroom and, turning quickly, I darted out the servants' entrance to the back stairs and up through the dark passages and the swinging door to my rooms, where I grabbed my cell phone. My hand shook as I punched Montero's office number. It rang interminably before a secretary answered.

"Department of Art and Archeology. Good morning."

"Is Professor Courtney there?"

His voice came on the line. "Courtney here."

"Monty. Can you come to my rooms right away?"

Jared's frame filled the doorway. I started nervously and dropped my phone. He picked it up, walked to the window, opened it, and threw the telephone out into the moat. I heard it splash. Then he shut the door and locked it before he turned back to me. "Who were you calling? Our friend the art thief?"

"What makes you think he will steal it?"

"You know as well as I do."

"But why?"

"Why indeed? To finance his little orphanage at Bluecove? Because the Courtney's have been pirates, robbers and smugglers running contraband in and out of that creek of theirs since the seventeenth century?" He bent over me. "Athena, you know I carry a gun. Now I want you to be very calm and very good. You are going to take the papers out of their hiding place and give them to me. Otherwise you have no chance of living to give them to Courtney."

"You wouldn't dare. You would never get away with it. Everyone would know it was you."

"I have planned this very carefully. I will take you back to the Fenderbog. Remember the snake that I told you about in New York? He is there, happily clearing the house of rodents. If you should still be alive, there would be an unfortunate accident. Otherwise, well the woods of the Fenderbog Road are filled with hunters. It is sad. Bodies are often found, usually months after the deer season."

I heard the sound of the jeep engine in the parking lot and the slam of the car door before the door of the castle opened.

Jared stood up straight and buttoned his blazer. The quick gesture of his hand to his chest, as if checking for a pen or cigarettes, might have seemed natural if I had not known about his gun. Through the open window we heard the orchestra begin a Beatles' medley.

A key turned in the lock, and Montero appeared in the doorway, as straight and silent as the man he confronted. The resemblance in bone structure and build was still striking. As Montero stepped forward, however, he seemed the taller of the two. I was reminded of the ability of an angry cat to double its size. Jared seemed to shrink. His hand went again to his chest but then fell to his side. The two men circled so that Montero had his back to the window and Jared was near the door.

"Hello, Cousin," he said.

"What brings you here?" said Montero. His voice carried easily over the music from the ballroom. Jared's pained smile became a rictus of such hate that my breath stopped. "Get out."

Jared took a step backward. His reply was inaudible because of the music.

"I said out."

"You will regret this, Monty." Jared said, still moving backwards, "until the day you die. Which will be soon."

"I have regretted your existence," Montero said, "since the week we were both born."

Jared's eyes burned into mine. "I'm sorry, Athena," he said. "Remember. Whatever happens, it will not be my fault." Then the mask was back. He bowed and left the room, closing the door behind him. Only then did I draw a deep breath.

"Thank God you came," I said. "Montero. Thank God. Just in time." I gave a laugh that sounded braver than I felt.

Montero stretched out his arms and pulled me to him. His heart was pounding under my head as he buried his hand in my hair, breathing hard. "It's all right now. It's all right," he murmured. After a while he sank onto the window seat, drawing me down beside him, pressing his rough cheek to my forehead. "I feel as if I had left a little lamb in the wolf's den. If anything had happened." He shuddered and buried his face in my neck for a minute. "But you're safe. You're safe with me." He was quiet again, and I rested warm and comfortable in his arms until I became aware that it was more than fright and relief that was causing my heart to race. I drew back and placed my hand on his cheek, pressing my hand into the waving hair that was turning silver at his temple. For a minute he imprisoned my hand under his. Then he restored it to me, and his quick smile flashed as he set me on my feet and stood, brushing the wrinkles from his clothes.

"Well. Stay away from that man. He has absolutely no...he's simply outside the civilized world, my dear. Good lord." He recoiled from his watch. "It's almost time for class. Here. I've messed up your hair and collar." He straightened both with a gentle hand, but his eyes avoided mind. "Come with me now and on the way you can tell me what happened." As he held the door for me, the orchestra began a waltz.

"Why was he there?" he asked as he backed the jeep around to face the causeway. He shot across it and through the narrow gate so swiftly that for a minute I couldn't speak. When he stopped for a red light on Harbor Street, I swallowed. "You're going to kill yourself doing that someday," I said. "You don't even wear a seatbelt. Suppose somebody shut that gate?"

"They never do," he answered. "Has Jared been making passes at you?" He shot me a quick glance. "No need to blush. He hits on every attractive woman who crosses his path. Always has. But here is what I need to know. Why ever did you let him into your room? You should never have let him in."

Something in his authoritative tone ignited my already inflamed nerves. "Why not?" I snapped. "I can think for myself, you know."

"It is my duty to protect you, Athena." His voice was steady, but I could see that he, too, was angry.

"I don't want to be protected," I blazed at him. "And it isn't normal protectiveness. It's over-protectiveness. You're the most domineering man I ever met. Worse than my father. Even with your own family. Maybe you're the lord of Bluecove and the king of Brightwater, but you've got no right to treat me like a brainless cog in your own self-centered universe."

He did not answer, keeping his eyes on the hill as he shifted into low gear and drove into the traffic, almost causing an accident behind us. I looked at the greying hair that waved at his temple and then followed his example and looked straight ahead, and we drove to the university as cold and separate as minutes before we had been warm and close.

CHAPTER TWELVE

Saturday was the day of the ball, and I was busy until evening helping the musicians and the caterers. Tables were set up in the great hall and the salons as well as the dining room.

The morning had dawned bright and warm with a southwest breeze, but in early afternoon the wind had dropped and the sky had darkened. As I stood at my window before changing out of my work clothes, I looked out at a sea as flat and dark as a slate slab beneath an iron sky. I opened the window and leaned out. I had never seen the tide so low. The air was still and cold, and still and cold were the pale barnacles and the rags of seaweed exposed by the retreat of the water down the dreary shore. I shivered and closed the window and drew the curtains against the brooding air.

"It's the weather that makes me feel like this," I said aloud and reached for my cellphone to check the weather forecast. But my pocket was empty. Jared had thrown my phone into the moat. There would be no more calling for help, even if Montero and I had not parted in anger.

Like a zombie, I walked to the closet and took down my new dress. My fingers were numb and cold as I struggled to fasten the hooks in back. I heard the muffled thud of the wind striking my window. The lights flickered. I drew back the curtains and saw that the sky was still grey, but now strangely lit, like a reflection from old pewter, and the surf had risen in great parallel ridges streaked with yellow foam. The sound came again. My hands trembled as I fastened my mother's earrings and tied her cameo on a black velvet ribbon around my neck. My lips were as pale as my cheeks. I put on makeup carefully.

Jared's knock came almost at once. He was wearing a well-cut dinner jacket and he carried a florist's box. I stepped out of the door and shut it behind me. He gave an approving nod. "You look enchanting, my dear."

"You look okay yourself," I snapped. "And I'm not your dear."

"Ouch. And I brought you a gardenia. Let me pin it on."

"I can manage." I took the flower from his hand, but my cold hands fumbled with it until he slipped his fingers under the material of my dress and secured it. I was relieved that I felt no reaction at all. His behavior of the day before had quenched any attraction between us. He might as well have been the cigar store Indian that, to my disenchanted eyes, he resembled. He left the box on the floor by the door and offered me his arm, but I pretended not to notice and walked ahead of him to the gallery and down the stairs to the hall, where crowds of people were beginning to gather.

Montero and William were waiting for me at the bottom of the stairs. William's eyes widened with pleased appraisal, but Montero's were somber. Emma, gleaming in gold satin, clung to his arm. His white tie and tails were freshly pressed but threadbare, as if handed down for generations. On his other side, Victor shone brightly, from his hair to his shoes.

"Yo, Athena," he approved, "awesome."

"Red is certainly your color," Emma vouchsafed.

"Will you save a waltz for me?" asked Montero.

"Of course."

The fire huddled low on the hearth and an acrid draught of smoke blew into the hall. Again the lights flickered. Montero tilted his head, listening. "It's the line storm," he said. "Gus was right."

"Then come," Jared said to me. "Let us go to dinner before the power fails and the causeway floods and we all have to go home."

"Do you think that will happen?"

"It has happened before."

At the table, William sat at my right and Victor across from me, from where he managed to meet my eye when one of his elders amused him. I realized when a well-timed nudge of his shoe against mine nearly caused me to lose my composure that he was closer to my age than his father was.

The meal was merry, with the Courtney's as entertaining as usual and Montero charming and expansive. Emma drank only a little and seemed genuinely happy. Beside me, Jared was silent and self-effacing. The candle flames streamed and smoked in the sudden draughts, and when the lights dimmed the jovial company applauded.

When the music began, Jared and I were among the first on the floor. He pressed me close, but I pushed him back with a strength that seemed to startle him. Soon William cut in, holding me at a courtly distance and moving slowly with his bad leg.

"He's bruised your gardenia," he observed with his lovely smile.

"Thanks for rescuing me."

"My pleasure indeed." Victor cut in next and stayed with me for the next dance, a rock beat more familiar to both of us than the earlier slow dancing. We danced until we were breathless, and there was a pattering of applause from our neighbors, who had formed a ring around us, before I relinquished him to a crowd of pretty young women in prom dresses like colorful body casts.

For the first time since college, I had a different partner for each dance. Elderly gentlemen, while two-stepping, recited the Greek they had learned at Harvard. Boys in rented tuxedos boogied with me. A retired admiral whizzed me down the room in a tango, and every time Jared began to dance with me, one of the Courtney's would cut in. Even the strange man in the wheelchair seemed to be part of the conspiracy, for he wheeled himself to my side at the refreshment table as Jared approached. "I am Silas Fender," he said with a New England accent like dry autumn leaves. "Will you sit out this dance with me?"

"Thank you. I would be delighted. I am all out of breath." With a powerful gesture, he drew forward one of the caterer's little gold chairs. I introduced myself and sat down beside him.

"Might I?" Jared inquired, bowing.

"Go away, Jared," said Silas. "This dance is mine. Dance with Emma. You have neglected her this evening." The side of Jared's face rippled. He faded into the crowd.

The pale face was turned straight ahead, tilted upward, presenting his expressionless profile as we sat in silence. I overheard a woman say to Maude Courtney, "Who's the little beauty with Si?"

"Monty's new assistant, Sophie Grey's daughter."

"That's who she reminds me of. Lucky Monty."

The music began.

"I have no conversation," said Silas Fender. "Let us listen to the music in peace," and so we did. When the orchestra struck up, *The Artist's Life*, Montero came to my side and bowed slightly to Silas. "May I?" Silas nodded in silence.

"Will you waltz with me, Athena?" He took my hand, and I looked up at him. "Such eyes," he said gently. "Why so sad?"

"I'm sorry," I said. "For being so awful. Yesterday afternoon."

He smiled as he led me out to the floor. "I'm the one who should be apologizing. After tonight I'll try to change."

We moved as one as the music swept us around the great room. When the orchestra stopped, Montero asked the leader to play *Tales from the Vienna Woods*, and we danced on. With the wine, the music; the strings of fairy lights like stars in the beautiful room, our perfectly matched motion, and his blue eyes resting on my face, for that brief time I was perfectly happy. All my sadness, loneliness and fear were swept away by the magic of the dance.

When we finally came to halt, I blurted out, "I love you."

Bending low to my ear so only I could hear him, he whispered, "I love you, too."

When it was over, William came up to us and said, "If you mean to go through with this announcement, Monty, this is the time."

"It's only ten-thirty."

"The water's up to the causeway. There's going to be a surge tide by midnight, and the power's already out in parts of the Point. We'll have to quit early." The lights dimmed again.

"All right. One moment please, I'll be right there. Athena, a word." Montero led me a few paces away and again leaned low for my ears only, "There are things I must do, but trust in me, please Athena, I will make it all right. I can't explain just yet." As he straightened to follow William he said, "Good bye, Athena." Montero kissed my cheek before moving off into the crowd.

"Could I have the last dance, at least," murmured Jared, materializing at my side.

"Yes. Sure." Distracted, I scarcely heard him.

William had stepped up to the microphone, and a silence fell as he tapped to test it. "Ladies and gentlemen," he said, and there was a general chuckle as if he had said something funny. He was clearly well-liked in Brightwater. "We want to thank you all for your marvelous attendance tonight. We have exceeded our fund raising goal once again." There was applause before he continued. "Unfortunately our weather experts tell us that once again this year we will have to stop the party early because of a line storm." There was an outbreak of talking followed by shushing as William continued. "But before we all leave to get over the causeway before it sinks, I would like to propose a toast."

There was another commotion. I noticed that the waiters were moving through the crowd with trays of champagne. Jared took two and gave one to me. William raised his own glass. His face was as white as his hair. "To the happiness of my nephew Monty and our dear Emma, who are announcing their engagement tonight." There was more applause and a call of, "Speech. Speech."

Montero's pained smile gave him a startling look of Jared, who stood so still that he hardly seemed to breathe. "To Emma. Health and happiness," Montero said. The orchestra struck up "The Anniversary Waltz", and Jared led me silently around the edge of the ballroom.

People were streaming out of the Castle, leaving Montero and Emma dancing almost alone, like the couple on top of some cosmic wedding cake. The wind thudded. The lights went out, leaving the flickering radiance of the fire and the candles. The music ended, and the stragglers shook hands with the engaged couple as they left.

As the lights went out, I was grateful for the darkness that allowed me to compose my features before the flickering candles could show my shock. *'Trust in me' he said, how can he profess to love me and be engaged to her?* As we approached the 'happy couple' I scrambled for something to say that wouldn't betray my inner turmoil.

"Congratulations, Professor Courtney," I said rather stiffly as Jared led me out. "Best wishes, Emma. Do you want me to stay for the clean-up?"

"No thank you, darling. The caterers will do everything. You look so pretty. You must always wear red."

"Thank you," I murmured. Jared kissed Emma's cheek and shook Montero's hand in silence, and in silence he walked me back to my door.

"Thanks for a lovely evening," I said mechanically.

"Even if once again your heart is broken?"

"I was sure it was you and Emma."

"I and Emma what? You needn't answer. Your color speaks for you. Well, I thought surely it was you and Monty. So once again we must console each other. Remember the song? *Put your arms...*"

"Jared," said Victor, looming up behind him. "Si is looking for you to help him into the car. Good night, Athena."

I slipped inside my door, where I stood grinding my knuckles into dry, smarting eyes. In my mind heard the voice of the fatuous undergraduate. *Aren't you just in love with him?*

"No," I said aloud. "I hate his gaudy two-timing guts." I groped my way to the candles we had used at the last power failure and lit them. I unhooked the red dress and let it drop in bright rings to the floor. Over the silly underwear that I had bought on that long-ago day, I put on grey flannel slacks and a sweater. Instead of the satin pumps, I put on woolen socks and my salt-streaked boots from Michigan. I pulled my suitcase and backpack out of my closet and filled them with my few clothes. The books I could send for later. My only other possession was the Athena, and suddenly I didn't care who had designs on her any more. I would go back home and live in peace, if it meant I had to scrub floors in Ann Arbor.

I knelt on the window seat and pressed my hot forehead to the cool glass. The causeway was under water. I was trapped on Howe's Island. I would have to wait at least three hours before I could escape and go home to my old life. There was no question of staying, of working with him when he was married to Emma. I had to be honest with myself. All the passion had been on my part. While I had thrown myself at him like an adolescent with a crush, he had shown no more than the protective affection of an old family friend. Or had his tenderness been deliberate exploitation of my feelings, which must have been all too obvious, in order to acquire the papers? One thing was certain. Whether or not I ever saw him again, I would never throw myself at him again. Never. Not ever.

Eventually I lay down on top of the bed and slept fitfully until a sound from the hall awoke me. It was still dark. A floorboard creaked not far from my door. I started up and let myself out into the corridor, moving sideways downstairs to the gallery.

I heard a creak from the ballroom parquet, then a whisper in the darkness from the direction of the ballroom. A gust of wind buffeted the windows and the chimneys howled in response. Under cover of the noise, I crossed the gallery into the ballroom. The air before me moved, as though someone had passed so close that our clothes had nearly brushed. Emboldened by terror, I moved quickly to the case of the Athena.

The night outside the window was lighter than the blackness within. She was silhouetted dimly, her shape more felt than seen, and beside her were two men.

I could not scream. I could scarcely think. There was no electricity. The alarm would not sound. There was no escape. Some blind instinct caused me to grasp the case so that nobody could hurt it without hurting me. A hand closed around my wrist. I began to struggle.

Suddenly, the lights went on, revealing my adversary as Victor, and the siren of the alarm went off. Victor, more startled than I, allowed me to shake off his grip.

"Damn it, Athena!" Montero had to shout above the siren. "Let go of that case."

"You!" I blazed back. "I trusted you."

"You've set off the alarm."

"It'll take them a while to get here," said Victor.

"Not Jared. It's hooked up at Emma's house as well as the police station. We'll have to change our plans. No hope of sailing to Boston now. Athena. Do you have a suitcase?"

"They're packed. I'm leaving tomorrow."

"Good. Is one small enough to carry on an airplane?"

I didn't answer.

"Hurry. We have no time."

"Are you crazy? Miss Adams was right. You're trying to steal the Athena."

"We're succeeding." Carrying the little statue, he propelled me ahead of him. "And we need you. You must do as I say."

In my room, he gave an approving grunt at the sight of my backpack on the window seat. "Open it up."

I unzipped it. "Can you make some room for her?" he said.

I took out some jeans, burning with rage under his gaze, and he wrapped the Athena in my nightgown, tucked her in among my clothes and zipped the backpack shut. He strapped it on to my shoulders — it was surprisingly heavy — and led me to the door. "Why were you leaving?" he asked as he hurried me down the corridor.

"Because I hate it here."

"I'm sorry. You'll understand soon. Believe me."

"Believe YOU!" I marched ahead of him so that he couldn't see my face.

"Do you have the keys?" I handed them to him. "And your passport?"

"It's in my pocket." I checked its bulk in my inside jacket pocket.

"Let's go. Gus is waiting."

"No he's not," Jared's voice rapped out. "He has been detained by the coast guard."

We whipped around to face him in the doorway. He was holding his revolver, and it was pointed at Montero. "Get out of the way, Athena," he said. "Or you'll get hurt, too." He held out his left hand to draw me to his side.

Instead, I threw myself between Montero and the gun. Jared froze for an instant, and we dove into the dining room, slammed the door, bolted for the breakfast room, and locked the door behind us. We heard a shot as Montero fumbled for the spring in the paneling. As the bookcase swung open, another shot blew the lock off the breakfast room door.

Victor's flashlight led our way down the circular staircase, but we heard Jared slam the door above, and he turned it off. The rocks were slimy underfoot. We unbarred the last door and crowded through.

"Good," said Montero, replacing the two-by-four on the other side. "That'll keep him busy." He opened the double doors to the water. The cold wind struck us. The tide was low. He took some oilskins and a life preserver from the hooks on the wall. They were so big that they fitted over my backpack, and they were stiff and reeked of linseed oil and mold. He buckled some latches quickly and then picked me up and put me over the side of the motorboat on the ramp. "Shove off," he said, and he and Victor pushed the boat down the ramp and boarded it. The waves snatched us, the motor exploded into life, and we roared away from the boathouse.

There was another shot. We ducked down.

"It'll be getting light soon," said Victor. We were taking the waves broadside, rocking close to the water. Victor was at the tiller.

"Head up," said Montero

We headed into the waves. Spray flew over the bow. It was salty and bitter cold. "Where to?" said Victor. All his boyish charm had dropped away, and he was grimly businesslike.

"Listen."

There was the sound of another motorboat behind us. We rose to the crest of a wave, and the beam of a searchlight swept over us. Shots rang out before we dropped into the trough. "That was the coast Guard," said Montero. "A warning shot. Jared's are closer."

The sky had greyed enough with the dawn that I could see the water around us. The next wave towered, sure to sink us, when miraculously we were once more on the top. From there we could see a sail nearby.

"It's Gus," Montero said. "To windward. We'll board her."

The motor roared. Spray flew like ice bullets. In the greyness, we stopped suddenly, now moving only vertically with the seas. There was a sound of canvas flapping as the sailboat pulled alongside.

"Over you go." I was catapulted into the hands of Gus Howe. Victor soon followed. "Cleat that line." Victor went forward and tied the sailboat to the motorboat. For a minute we were towed swiftly into the wind, the sail flapping loudly. Then our boat plunged as Montero came aboard. "Cast off."

The empty motorboat roared away, and we bore off, heeling over with the sudden silence of sail. Soon we heard another engine, and the cutter passed us, following the motorboat.

"Jared said the coast guard got you," Montero said, still breathing hard. Gus chuckled from his place at the tiller.

"We'll all be in our graves, Monty," he said, "the day the feds get Augustus Howe."

CHAPTER THIRTEEN

I shivered in the dawn wind, colder than I had ever been before. The seas continued high. A sudden gust dowsed the lee rail, and we could see the centerboard.

"Good thing it's too rough for helicopters," said Gus. "You still bound for Boston?"

"No. The alarm went off."

"Christ. How'd that happen?"

"Athena here." He spoke with ironic pride. "She was right there when the power went back on."

"I guess that power failure wasn't such a lucky break after all. Still, we should have let you in on it," he added to me.

"Too late now," said Montero. "Put in at Bluecove, Gus."

"Your place? That's the first place they're going to look."

"They're going to look all over the Point," said Montero, "and I feel safer on my own ground."

"Okay. The pier?"

"No. Too exposed. Go up the creek under the viaduct."

"Guess there's been Courtney's sneaking stuff up that creek for three hundred years."

I began to shiver again. I realized that my impulsive gesture at the Castle had put me irrevocably on the side of these pirates, outside the law.

"You can take out those reefs, boys," Gus said at length. Montero and Victor untied the points, letting out the sail, adjusting the halyards. The water churned in our wake.

"I'm going in on the starboard tack," Gus said. "Monty, the centerboard. Vic, up forward. Ready about."

"Get down," Monty said, drawing me to the floorboards.

"Hard a lee." The great boom swung across, the hull tilted again, Montero pulled me up to the other side. I could see the headlands and beach of Bluecove, suddenly very near. The wind diminished as we approached the shelter of the land. Gus looked up at the sail, which was lulling a little. In near silence we slipped into the creek and up to the viaduct. The sail grew slack. Victor said, "Two feet. One foot." The centerboard thumped. Montero pulled it up. Beyond the viaduct, a stone jetty tossed up spray.

"Here, Gus," Montero said. He lept lightly on to the rocks and held the boat off them. "Over you go, Athena. Okay, Victor. Ready, Gus?"

"Shove off."

"Thanks. I'll see you."

"If you stay out of jail. Take it easy." The old man tipped his hat to me, let out the boom, and ran before the wind out to sea, with no sound but the water splashing against the hull.

Montero half dragged me up the bank to the railroad tracks and then off to a dirt road that ran between stone walls to the lawn of Bluecove. I heard the sound of an engine, and by now the cloudy morning was light enough for us to see the coast guard cutter on the water. We crossed the lawn and the terrace, and Victor bolted the back door behind us. Following his example, I shook off the stiff oilskins and life preserver and hung them on a peg behind the door. I felt as if I had shivered until the bones had come loose from my joints.

"Take off those wet socks," Montero ordered. He rummaged through a laundry basket in the corner. "These should be small enough. My nephew Willy left them when he went back to school last week." They were wool, and they insulated my feet from the wet boots.

In the distance we heard the sound of sirens.

"We're out of time," said Montero, looking around as if for an escape. "I'm too damned visible. Wait." He stared at me and left the kitchen. A minute later we heard Maude's theater-filling voice from the next room. "You can't possible send her out alone."

"We have no choice," Montero replied. "Besides, she's fearless. You should have seen her stand up to Jared. Dare him to shoot her."

The sirens were closer. The mother and son returned, Maude in a sweat suit. She quickly turned to me. "You're my grandson, Willy Robinson, and I'm getting you on the bus back from school and home to Boston. Off with those earrings." I took out the gold keepers and put them in my pocket. She slid the backpack off my shoulders and snatched a dishtowel from the rack and some safety pins from a drawer. "Take off your sweater and wrap this around you. Flatten that chest." She did it for me with the sure fingers which had often transformed a well-endowed soprano into Cherubino. I was aware of Victor glancing at my red lace bra and Montero tactfully averting his eyes. She whipped a white shirt out of the laundry basket and buttoned it onto me. "A necktie, boys," she snapped. "And Willy's blazer and cap. Rain jacket, too." She put them on me, restored my backpack, ran a comb under the faucet to discipline my hair into a boyish ducktail and jammed on a cap with a Brightwater Academy school crest.

Montero spoke quickly. "The police are coming down the lane. There's a back road to the highway. Leave the bridge to your left and turn right. When you get to the main road, take the first bus to Brightwater, and from the terminal take a bus to Boston. Go to the international charter terminal, where you will find a school tour headed by Badger's daughter Debby. She has a ticket and will take you to Athens. Here's the itinerary, the flight and tour group number and a hundred dollars American and a hundred Euros. Do you have any money?"

"Some."

"Okay. If you have to spend it, I'll pay you back. Once you're in Athens, go to the Hotel Ermou on Metropoleou Street and check in and wait for me there. If I don't come,"

"If you don't come?"

"Don't wait for more than twelve hours. Go on to Agios Titos, to the village museum. Your Uncle's the curator. He'll know what to do."

Through the windows, the rotating lights of the police car threw red and blue beams on the walls. There was a pounding on the back door, and a shout of "Police!"

Montero opened the door. "Yes, officer?"

"Mr. Courtney?"

"You know me, Ben."

"Sorry, Monty. We've got a warrant to search this house."

"Now. Do you have everything?" Maude said to me. "Run along to the bus, then, and give our love to your mom. Uncle Monty's got to talk to the nice police officer. Say good bye to the family." She and Victor hugged me, but I eluded Montero's avuncular embrace, true to the vow I had made in the agony of the night.

"Still Oscar the grouch," he smiled. "Bye, Willy."

"Just like my kid. Copies Oscar the grouch. Hates to be hugged," said the policemen.

I said, "Bye Grandma," and slipped out the back door, attempting a macho walk while trying to make the heavy backpack look natural. Halfway across the lawn, I turned and waved at the white-haired figure in the doorway. She waved back, and I strode to the bridge and turned right. The road wound into the woods. As I lost sight of the house behind the trees, a rabbit bounded across the road in front of me. A blue jay swooped close to my head, crying "Thief! Thief!" The backpack, with its burden of twenty-five hundred year old gold, hurt my shoulders. I wondered how I would get it through airport security and two customs inspections.

Soon I heard the traffic from the main road. There was a steep hill ahead of me. The rocks were loose and the footing bad after the night's storm, but ahead of me was the highway. Out of the shelter of the trees, I felt the wind whip fine rain into my face. The wait seemed interminable before the bus came. I handed the driver the ticket Mrs. Courtney had given me.

"Staying with the Courtney's?" His eyes flickered from my school cap to my necktie. I felt the blood leave my face, but I said nothing. The brakes hissed, the door shut, we swung out into the highway.

"Not many people live down here at Bluecove," the driver said. I picked my way, swaying, to the middle of the empty bus, where I sat looking at the rain slick pavement and the grey sky and sea beyond.

In the bus terminal, the clock said nine o'clock. I took a schedule out of the rack and sat on the bench, where I took from my inside pocket the wallet into which I had stuffed Montero's itinerary. It was for a charter flight that left Boston at 4:00 p.m., nonstop to Athens. The schedule said that a bus left Brightwater via New Stoke at 10:00 and arrived in Boston at 1:00. I snapped the wallet shut with a smile. I would have plenty of time to get from the bus station to Logan Airport.

But the man at the ticket window shook his head. "Sorry, kid." His puzzled eyes flickered from my necktie to my hair, which in the rain had curled forward to frame my face. "The next bus to Boston leaves at one, arrives at four."

"But the schedule says ..."

He took it from me and pointed at the letters ESH. "See here. That means except Sundays and holidays, and this is Sunday."

"But I've got to catch a four o'clock flight from Boston. Is there another bus line?"

"Nope." He turned away but seemed to think better of it. "Look. Uh. Kid. You old enough to drive?"

"Yes."

"Maybe you can rent a car. There's Hertz across the street and Snyder's down the block."

"Thanks." I hurried out into the wind and rain, pulling off the necktie and stuffing it into my pocket. The Hertz agency looked too visible, so I hurried to the more obscure Snyder's Budget Economy at the shabby end of the street, between a bar and a purveyor of fried darns. The man quoted me a flat rate which seemed neither budget nor economical. After glancing at my license and swiping my credit card, he pointed through the dirty window to the parking lot, where two elderly Hondas were parked. Judging by the seagull damage, they had been there for a long time.

"I'll take the red one," I said. He handed me the keys.

On the radio, the music stopped and a mellifluous voice said, "And now for the headlines of the hour. A dramatic announcement from the Brightwater Police..."

I hitched up my backpack and fled through the back door. I locked myself and the Athena into the car and fumbled with the ignition and gearshift. The battery was low. The starter labored for a long time before the engine turned over. When it finally began to move, the car had a maddeningly slow pick up. In the rearview mirror I saw Snyder run out to the sidewalk and then down the block, waving for me to stop. I turned the corner to the main street and headed out of Brightwater.

I turned on the radio, and the voice said, "And now for the weather. Rain and northeasterly winds of gale force continuing today. Storm warnings are up from Eastport to Block Island ..." Frantically I pushed buttons but got only music and sermons. The news was over.

Once out of the city, I sped down the entrance ramp to the superhighway, but when I came in sight of the Brightwater Bridge, I saw that it was blocked by police cars, their lights flashing. I exited onto the Fenderbog Road to the old bridge. As before, there were red flags flying from the superstructure, but this time a barricade with red winking lights proclaimed ROAD CLOSED.

On the right was parked a Cadillac limousine. It was many years old, for it had great tailfins and a chrome grin above its front bumper. Against it lounged two men who, when I stopped, stood up and sauntered toward my car. I kept the motor running.

The first man was in his forties, deeply tanned, with a scar across his chin beneath a smile that showed two gold teeth. One ear was pierced by a gold hoop. The younger man had black hair to his shoulders and prominent cheekbones that gave him and oriental look. His jaw hung loose, and his eyes were as empty as the windows of a vacant house. Both men wore yellow oilskins.

"Excuse me," I said, opening the window a half inch. "Would I be able to cross the bridge?"

The older man looked around the inside of the car until he saw the backpack, and he stared at that before he spoke to the boy. "What do you think, Jim?"

"Uh yuh," said Jim, and he gave a high, loud laugh.

"He says you can make it," said the man, "but you got to pay the toll."

"How much?" I asked, annoyed.

"Four bits. You got two quawtas?"

I fumbled in my wallet, and, opening the window a few inches more, laid the silver in his brown palm.

"The brakes," said Jim.

"He says watch out for the brakes. You got water on the bridge because the piers have sunk some, so dry out your brakes on the other side."

"Thank you," I said. They moved the barricade, and I closed my window and drove on to the bridge. The water flew up on both sides of the car like a bow wave. In the middle of the bridge, as I peered at the front of the car, I saw a puff of steam. I glanced down at the dashboard and saw that the temperature had risen above the middle line of the gage. I stepped on the gas and sped between walls of water to the other side. Once on dry land again, I pumped the brakes and slowed down. In the mirror, I saw the Cadillac crossing the bridge in a cloud of spray. I speeded up, but it kept up with me. The temperature gage was almost at the top. A red light on the dashboard went on. Steam was now streaming from under the hood. The Cadillac sounded its horn and pulled out and passed me, roaring ahead until a quarter of a mile up the road it stopped crosswise, blocking my way.

I put on the brakes. There was a muffled explosion under the hood, and steam poured over my windshield, blinding me. I pulled over to the shoulder and stopped.

As the steam cleared away, I saw the two men approaching. They were smiling. I turned the ignition key. There was no response. The engine was dead.

CHAPTER FOURTEEN

The older man tapped on my window, and again I opened it a half inch. "You Athena Grey?" he asked.

I swallowed. "How do you know my name?"

"You work for Monty Courtney, right?"

"Yes."

"We're friends of Monty. He sent us to help you out. I'm Jasper and this is my son Jim. He's not smart, but he's a genius with machines." The boy had gone to the front of the car and opened the hood. He came back holding a broken fan belt. "You get this car from Snyder's?" asked Jasper.

I nodded.

"Figures. You got the statue?"

"What statue?"

"Look, Miss Grey. We haven't got time to be funny. When's your flight from Boston?"

"Four o'clock."

"Okay. We got time. We'll leave Jim here to get the car back to Snyder's and we'll make sure you get a refund." He spoke quickly to Jim in a language I didn't understand, but it sounded Latin based. As I still hesitated inside the locked car, Jasper's eyebrows lowered and his nostrils flared. "You don't trust us? You want maybe identification from the F.B.I? Well, listen, lady, what the hell else are you going to do?"

"You're right," I said and opened the car door.

"Out we go," said Jasper. He took my wrist in a grasp so tight that it slowed the circulation in my hand. He took the keys that had been in the ignition and unlocked the gate into a driveway choked with brambles and weeds beneath an arch of elms, dripping in the rain. The gate closed behind us, silent on oiled hinges. The weeds caught at my feet as Jasper dragged me along. I was grateful for my sturdy Michigan boots.

Before us stood an eighteenth century mansion, enormous and rambling among its many wings. The roofline sagged between great chimneys, and some windowpanes were broken or mended with brown paper. A Victorian grape arbor extended from the left side of the facade, and in the shelter of the trailing bare tendrils, Silas Fender sat in his wheelchair, wrapped in shawls, lifting his pale face to the sky.

"Where's Jared's stinking snake?" asked Jasper.

"Locked in the rose garden," Silas replied, not turning his head or acknowledging my presence. Jasper grunted and dragged me through the front door into the hall, an impressive space lighted by an electric bulb dangling by a wire from the ceiling. A staircase swept upward from a newel post, a hand carved pineapple, the symbol of hospitality. On the walls, Chinese tea paper was spotted with mold and centuries of handprints. On a Persian rug, worn to the knots, a hound nursed several whelps that wriggled greedily against her skinny ribs. She raised her head and snarled at me. With a gesture oddly homey in this bizarre atmosphere, Jasper tossed the keys on to the front hall chest, from which the inlay curled like shavings. He kicked the dog in the head until she was silent.

"Jared?" Jasper called.

The door at the end of the hall opened, and Jared Fender stepped out. "Thank you, Cousin," he said. "That will be all."

Jasper clattered to the back of the house in his steel tipped workboots. In the split second while Jared turned to open another door, I whipped out my hand to grab the keys. Jasper's grip had left my hand so numb that it nearly fumbled, but as Jared gestured me into the room I felt their weight safe in my blazer pocket against my hip.

"I hope," said Jared, "that my cousins didn't frighten you, Athena, but you didn't plan to take the Fenderbog Road without meeting the Fenders, did you?"

The room into which he had led me was small and as shabby as the hall, but a fire in the fireplace dispelled the chill of the day. There was a little armchair covered with rags of rose silk and a tiny loveseat to match. On the mantelpiece, its blind eyes directed toward me, stood a marble head of powerful workmanship. I stepped forward involuntarily.

"Skopas?" I asked. He nodded. Next to the head stood a crystal ball, grey with dust.

"My Grandmother's," Jared said. "The one I told you about. Madam Ursula. And the head, of course, is the one I just got from the collector in Brazil. I am going to sell it to a museum for him as part of the same deal by which I will receive several million dollars for the Athena."

"You'll never get away with it," I said.

"Get away with what? Don't forget, my dear, that it is you and your friends who are the art thieves. The Athena belongs legally to Emma, and she wishes me to sell it. What a pity that you didn't join us willingly. You would have been rich. As it is, you have saved us much trouble. Open the suitcase. Now. No." He held up his hand. "Wait. She should be here for this occasion."

"Who is she?"

"You will soon see." He edged toward the door.

I let my eyes fly to the French windows which formed one wall of the little room. They opened onto a small garden surrounded by a stone wall about seven feet high. The garden was filled with a bare tangle of rosebushes and a cherry tree. A movement caused my blood to freeze. A snake about eleven feet long was coiled around one branch and down the trunk of the tree.

"Another acquisition from my Brazilian friend," Jared explained. "The largest pit viper in the western hemisphere. The bushmaster. There is only one other in captivity, so it is a fascinating specimen for research. There is so little known about them. Their victims don't live to reach the hospital. What a fitting end for a classical archeologist. Its scientific name is Lachesis — one of the three fates, was she not?" He let himself out the door, and I heard the key turn in the lock.

The chill that had gripped me at the sight of the snake grew more intense until I felt colder than I had in the boat at dawn. The lock turned again, and I whipped around to encounter not Jared but Silas Fender, who rolled into the room on silent wheels and closed the door noiselessly behind him. Without speaking, he reached into the breast of his blue blazer and drew out a pearl handled pistol, the twin of Jared's. My teeth chattered, and when I unclenched them, my breath formed a cloud before my eyes.

As I stared at it, the cloud sank into the silk armchair and formed itself into a beautiful woman, neither young nor old, with chains of coins around her neck. "Madam Ursula," I said.

"Run. Quickly," she answered. Her voice was at once silent and perfectly clear, like remembered music. "Lachesis wants only the heat of the fire. The giver of lots will not interfere with your destiny. Only with another's."

"But how..."

"Run," she repeated. I felt again the warmth of the room and my heart pounding and my breath coming hard as if I awoke from a nightmare. She was gone.

I turned toward Silas, who held the gun with two hands, pointed at my head. "Go," he whispered. "Go. Or come with us."

The French window was unlocked. I opened it and bolted for the garden wall. The snake poured itself down the tree and across the windowsill. I threw the backpack upwards with all my strength. It hit the top of the wall and teetered for a minute and then crashed into the weeds on the other side. With a fleeting memory of my failed radochla, I jumped for a high branch of the cherry tree. My shoulders took my weight, and I flung myself at the wall, scrambled over, and fell down on the other side, hearing the keys clank in my pocket as I hit the ground.

Shouldering the backpack, I ran stumbling through the weeds to the front gate, which I unlocked and then locked behind me. The Cadillac was still there. I locked myself into it, moved the seat forward so that I could reach the accelerator, and started the powerful engine. I rocked out of the dirt road, but the way to the Fenderbog Road was blocked by Snyder's Honda, with Jim Fender at the wheel. He swerved aside as I approached and leaned out the window, staring with his empty innocent eyes. "Danger, lady," he cried in his high voice. "Watch out! Danger!" I floored the gas pedal and passed him, and the speedometer rose to eighty as I sped silently out the Fenderbog Road.

It was two-thirty when I parked the car in the lot at Logan Airport and walked rapidly toward the terminal. "Take your luggage, kid?" The porter had his hand on my pack.

"No thanks. It's a carry on."

The mechanical doors leapt apart at my approach, and the big board told me that my flight was on time and scheduled to leave from a gate at the charter concourse.

The line at the security gate was slow. Finally, I put my shoes, blazer, jacket and backpack in the dishpan on the conveyor belt and took my place behind a short, dark man in a business suit. The buzzer sounded as he went through, and the security guard took him aside and ran a metal detector over his clothes.

I stepped through the checkpoint and looked back at the screen over the conveyor belt. There was my pack and, in it, outlined as clearly as in a drawing, the Brightwater Athena, helmeted and resting one hand on her shield, the little victory extended in the other. The security woman stopped the conveyor belt and studied the image.

"Real cunning," she said. "What is it?"

"It's an old statue," I said. "A family keepsake. I'm taking it to my Giagia, my grandma in Greece." The belt started again. My pack and jackets and shoes came out from inside the machine, I quickly put them back on and strode down the concourse.

"Police are looking for a young woman of about twenty-five, dressed to resemble the alleged suspect's nephew, a boy of twelve named William Robinson. The woman is five feet tall and weighs about one hundred pounds. She was last seen wearing the school uniform of Brightwater Academy..." The woman on the television screen was speaking into a microphone, and behind her rambled the house at Bluecove. She had underestimated my height by two inches and my weight by a good ten pounds. The mistake might work in my favor.

I looked behind me. In the distance, beyond the security checkpoint but easily recognizable by their height and dramatic appearance, came Jared Fender and Emma Trapper. For an instant I was frozen, but then I dodged sideways down the international charter concourse and dove into the nearest ladies' room. It was empty, and I stood for a minute pondering my next move, since my impulse had been simply to hide. Where was Madam Ursula when I needed her? Where were Mr. Badger's daughter and her school tour?

I had never felt so alone. I sent up a fervent Greek Orthodox prayer, making the sign of the cross as my mother had taught me, right shoulder first, before I set about changing my appearance. First I unpinned Mrs. Courtney's dishtowel and threw it in the trash.

Two girls came in to fix their hair in front of the mirrors. They looked at me, startled, and whispered to each other as I made up my face, put back my earrings, and opened my pack, carefully digging for my skirt and shoes and pantyhose while concealing the Athena. A struggle into these garments, a gold brooch at the collar of Willy's shirt and a quick combing to free my hair completed my change from androgyny to feminine respectability.

"At first we thought you were a guy," the tall black girl said. She was slim and elegant with a natural haircut and dangling gold earrings.

"I go, Diane, that's a GUY," giggled the equally tall blonde girl.

"And I'm like. Yeah. Right. A guy in here. But then when you started to change clothes I go, 'No. I think she's a teacher, Biffy.' Are you a teacher?" said Diane.

"Maybe a gym teacher," suggested Biffy. "A lot of them look like guys."

"Actually, I'm a Latin teacher."

"No kidding." They looked at each other with more excitement than had been inspired by my epicene appearance. "You've got to come and meet Badge."

"She'll freak."

"Are you going to Greece?"

"Do you want to come with us to Greece?'

"Sister Mott got sick."

"Just like her. Badge doesn't want to do this alone."

"We hope she doesn't call the head. Like call the whole trip off."

"So we don't even get a refund. Because of the charter."

"My Mom and Dad will be so mad."

They propelled me out of the washroom and into the presence of a young woman, thin and bespectacled, with brown hair hanging straight to her shoulders, who sat amidst a mountain of expensive luggage and a crowd of girls all as handsome and exuberant as Biffy and Diane.

"Miss Badger," Biffy said, "we found you another Latin teacher."

Miss Badger tucked a strand of hair behind one ear and raised her eyes wearily to mine. Her eyelashes were so long that they nearly touched the lenses of her glasses. She would have been pretty if she had not looked as if somewhere in her career as classics mistress her fire had gone out. "Hello. I'm Debby Badger, from Star of the Sea Convent School. I hope these girls haven't been bothering you."

I hesitated for a minute but then hazarded revealing the name on my passport. "Athena Grey," I said, extending my hand. "Your students say that you are looking for a Latin teacher."

"What have you two been up to?" Miss Badger asked.

"We thought," Diane began.

"That she might want to take the Mott's place. So we don't have to cancel ..."

"And lose the refund."

Debby rolled her eyes heavenward. "You GIRLS. I don't know what to do with you. We've already arranged for a sub. He's on his way. He'll be here in a minute."

The announcement brought an excited response from the group. "He?"

"A guy?"

"Is he cute?"

"How old?"

"Probably real old."

I drew Debby aside and dropped my voice. "Montero Courtney?" I asked. "He told me to meet the daughter of Mr. Bartholemew Badger." Her eyes widened behind the thick lenses as they swept over my appearance.

"You're that Athena Grey. What was I thinking? I guess I just had my mind set on seeing a tall older man. Do you have... "

I pulled the ticket and itinerary out of my breast pocket and handed it to her, and she nodded, perusing it. "There's no problem, I hope," she said.

"Well, only temporarily."

She looked at my backpack. "Is that it?"

I nodded.

"God! I'd love to see it."

"Can you explain what's going on?" I murmured. "I just got involved in this by accident."

"Dad and Monty Courtney cooked this up as a way of getting ... your package through customs and security."

"Of course. School tours are cleared ahead of time by the couriers to keep them from missing their connections."

"What are you guys whispering about?" demanded Biffy.

"Excuse me, Miss Badger," Debby corrected in a reflex I admired, for I had yet to acquire it.

"Excuse me, Miss Badger," the girl echoed good naturedly.

"This is Miss Grey, our new substitute."

Giggles ran around the circle of girls like a chime of bells. "You said it was a guy."

"She looked like a guy."

"You should of seen her."

"In the john."

"We thought she was a guy."

"Ladies. Please," said Debby. "Mr. Courtney couldn't make it, so Miss Grey is doing us a great favor by taking his place."

"Thank you, Miss Grey," chorused the girls in school singsong.

"Charter number five-twelve for Athens, Cairo and Tel Aviv now boarding at Gate Five," the loudspeaker said. "Please have your boarding pass and passport ready."

"Okay, ladies. Line up. You lead," Debby said as we fell into the chaperone configuration. I'll bring up the rear and do the count. I've got the tickets."

"The students of the Star of the Sea Seminary will board first," said the loudspeaker, and another peal of laughter greeted the misnomer.

"Athena Grey. Miss Athena Grey. Please report to the nearest courtesy phone," said the paging system. I kept my gaze straight ahead as the official at the desk scanned my boarding pass, examined my passport, and then smiled and waved me by. I boarded the airplane, still not breathing normally.

"Star of the Sea?" The steward led me to our block of seats in the middle of the airplane. "The teachers want to sit together? They usually do. I'll put your pack up. Oof! What've you got there? Bricks?'

"Books," I said, firmly keeping my grasp on the handle. "And I'll keep it under the seat in front of me. Thank you."

"All present and accounted for," said Debby, arriving at my side. "You want the window?"

"No, thanks. I'll take the aisle." I finished wedging the pack in place, and we strapped ourselves into our seats.

"Kyrioi kai kyriai," said the voice from the air, and I gave an involuntary jolt, expecting an announcement of the greatest art theft since the kidnapping of the Mona Lisa. But it was only the flight attendant explaining in Greek the proper use of seat belts, oxygen masks, and flotation devices. As I listened I was suddenly overwhelmed by the fatigue of the last twenty-four hours and a desolate sense of the seriousness of my situation.

    The airplane began to taxi out to the runway. The engines roared. The landing gear thumped. We were airborne; and, for the moment at least, Jared and Emma were still on the ground.

CHAPTER FIFTEEN

"Did you ever hear of Badger Steel?" Debbie was saying above the roar of the engines.

"Of course. I come from Detroit."

"Well, that's my Dad. He wanted me to go into engineering, but, you know, all I really want is to meet some nice guy that wouldn't mind sharing Daddy's money. I mean, I had a million dollars settled on me my twenty-first birthday. So I got a car. I mean, how much can a high school teacher spend? I tried to be a playgirl, but it was so boring that I went back to my old boarding school and they gave me a job."

The steward leaned over to unlatch our tables and place before each of us a tray set with mounds of international cuisine and a half bottle of wine.

"But Dad acted proud that I could do anything on my own, I guess. And I know he's happy that I got into Latin and Greek classics because he's always had this hobby of archeology. I mean he has all these works of art in his villa on Crete. Do you know the Badger Athlete? The one in all the art books? He's right there in the front hall. And Dad's been dying to get your little statue as long as I can remember. He set up this foundation to support research in Latin and Greek. Can you believe that? The Badger Foundation?"

"Oh yes. I've heard of it," I said. "They financed the William Courtney Expedition. Which reminds me. I've been dying to know how you got involved in this adventure."

"I've been wondering about you."

"You first. But keep your voice down. You never know." She obligingly leaned closer to me.

"You know Monty Courtney?"

"Slightly," I said, with a feeling that my heart was aching like an old war wound in bad weather.

"Isn't he a darling? Anyway, he was talking with my dad on his last visit to Crete about ... about your statue, and they were worrying about the problem of how to get it back. It was stolen, you know, from the little museum in Agios Titos, about a bazillion years ago, and both Monty and my dad have this mission to get it back. Anyway, I had just come back from chaperoning one of those student tours and mentioned how the couriers get you through customs by clearing you ahead of time and I'd be happy to do it. Of course Monty wouldn't hear of letting me do it, so he planned to come along. And, of course, then we had to have Sister Mott. You can't have a guy chaperone without a nun along." Debby giggled wryly. "Then you showed up. I hope he's okay."

"I hope so, too," I said, and we both lapsed into a worried silence.

"Someone from the Athens school will be with the courier to meet us," Debby said at length. "The Star of the Sea nuns are one of the few orders who have a school in Athens. Even Sacred Heart doesn't have a school there. I'm not quite sure what to tell her."

"Why not tell the truth?" virtuously responded this international art thief.

"Hmm." She meditated as we sipped our Greek wine. "What truth exactly?"

"That a passing Latin teacher volunteered to take Sister Mott's place to ensure a safe trip for the students. Then I will politely fade away and take a cab to Monty's hotel."

"What a brain," sighed Debby. "Shows the benefit of a classical education. We're going from Athens to Crete, the Minoan ruins at Knossos and then down to Agios Titos and then on to the caves at Matala. If you need anything, this will tell you where to find us."

"Thanks," I said, slipping the paper she handed me into my inside pocket with my passport.

Debby's gentle flow of conversation continued to wash over me as I enjoyed my first meal since the museum ball. As we flew into the night, I fell into a deep sleep until a few hours later when we flew into the morning, and I was awakened by the sunrise over the Alps.

It was full morning when the plane landed in Athens. I was aware of an ache in my right shoulder as I once again shouldered my burden of ancient gold and ivory. The girls, rumpled and sleepy after the short slumber that had followed their night of chattering and giggling were roused and marshalled off the airplane and onto the packed little bus which conveyed us to the terminal, where they were reunited with their impressive luggage. As the other passengers lined up for the customs inspection, a tall young woman carrying a sign with the name of a student tour travel agency introduced herself, shook hands with Debby and me, spoke with the customs official, and diverted us from the queue and under a barricade. In the distance, I saw a nun approaching, wearing a habit like the uniform of an old fashioned English nanny.

"Well, I guess you'll be okay," I said. "I'll be off now." Returning Debby's quick hug, I assumed my burden and beat a quick retreat into the crowd.

A line of taxicabs was waiting at the curb, and I gave the driver of the nearest one the address of Montero's hotel in the Plaka. The cab driver had bright eyes and a jaunty moustache, and he drove at a speed that would have made pursuit reckless if not impossible. Where an American would have put on the brakes, he leaned on the horn; and we hurtled through the suburbs unopposed.

Suddenly at the end of the street, I saw the walls of the Acropolis, more familiar to me from my years of study than the face of a friend, and above it against the Greek sky the Parthenon. Within those springing pillars had stood the long since destroyed Athena Polias, executed from the model that still lay safe in my pack.

With horn blasting, the taxi plummeted into an open square. We passed the Parliament House guarded by evzones still in their blue winter tunics. Then we turned down toward the banks and commercial buildings which rose above the sidewalk cafes of the vast space.

"Sindagma," said the driver. "Constitution Square." I nodded, mute. I was eager to keep a low profile. We passed the cathedral and entered a steep, narrow street which led to the cobbled alleyways of the oldest quarter of Athens, the Plaka, under the rock wall of the Acropolis. Pedestrians and motorcycles leapt aside at our approach. We stopped finally at the entrance to a tall hotel.

The lobby was small and dark and paved with marble. The proprietor, an Egyptian who spoke the Greek of Alexandria, told me that there was indeed a reservation for Professor Courtney, who stayed there whenever he was in Athens. The cost was reasonable, but he would have to take my passport. He assured me he would return it in a few hours. I had no choice but to surrender it, praying that my name was not yet on Interpol's list.

An ancient elevator took me to the second floor to a room sparsely furnished with blonde wood and faded chintz. The French doors opened on to a narrow balcony which overlooked the front entrance. I shut the door and put on the chain bolt. Then with a sigh of relief I kicked off my dress shoes, which under the weight of my pack had become torture devices, and quickly stripped off the rest of my clothes.

In the marble bath, luxuriously at odds with the slight seediness of its surroundings, I washed the Atlantic Ocean from my skin and hair and the kinks from my bones and muscles. Greatly refreshed, I changed into clean underwear and then my sweater and grey flannels, Willy's woolen socks, and my boots, still damp from the boat ride of two nights before.

Before I closed my pack, I unwrapped from my white nightgown the small figure which had come so far from Brightwater with me. Her eyes in the ivory face gazed back at me with a monumental serenity which inspired a similar calm in my own heart. For the first time since I had blocked Jared's aim, I felt secure and firm in my purpose. She and I had come a long way together. Whatever my present feelings for Montero Courtney, my destiny was inextricably linked with that of the Brightwater Athena and had been since I had been named for her by my parents in my infancy. Although she was mine, I had a stronger sense that I was hers.

I covered her again and closed and locked the backpack before I stretched out on the bed. With my feet resting on the pack, I yielded to jet lag and fell into a restless sleep. I dreamt, as I had so often, of Agios Titos, before the bright vision yielded to nightmare images of pursuit and danger, and I awoke with a start, my heart pounding I looked at my watch. It was afternoon. He had said not to wait more than a day. I arose and moved to the French windows, where I raised my eyes to the Acropolis, the Erichtheum and Parthenon visible in the blue haze which hangs over Athens more thickly every year. Then I lowered my eyes to Metropoleou Street below me and immediately shrank back into the shadows of the room.

I had seen Jared Fender and Emma Trapper crossing the street below me. He had a grasp on her upper arm, and they were entering the front door of the Hotel Ermou. I sat on the bed and picked up the telephone, which was answered by the proprietor.

"Yes, Miss Grey?" Mentally cursing the fact that Jared, standing there as he doubtless was, would hear my name, I asked to be connected with the Star of the Sea Convent School.

"Is that 'Star' or `Aster', Miss Grey?"

"I don't know," I snapped.

"Ah yes. Here we are. The name is in English. Shalt I ring it?"

"Nai. Eucharisto."

"Parakalo."

After an eternity of buzzing sounds, a female voice said, "Star of the Sea. Kalespera." There were footsteps in the corridor outside my door. "Despoinis Debby Badger, parakalo," I hissed into the phone. There was a knock on my door, and I heard Emma's voice.

"Athena? Athena, we know you're in there. Open the door."

"Kalespera," came Debby's voice on my phone. "Eimi Despoinis Badger. Melata Anglika?"

"Debby. It's me. Athena Grey," I whispered.

There was more knocking. "Be reasonable, Athena," Jared said. "We want to make you an offer. A share in the proceeds. It is a GREAT deal of money."

Another door opened down the hall, and an American accent complained, "Pipe down, wouldja? We got jet lag."

"Are you okay?" Debby's voice was so loud that I feared my adversaries would hear her. "This is a terrible connection. Want me to call back?"

"She could have escaped," Emma said outside the door. "Perhaps by the balcony."

"The room is in Courtney's name," said Jared. "If we wait downstairs we will meet one or the other."

I heard their footsteps retreating down the corridor and then the groan of the elevator. "Debby. When does your tour go to Knossos?"

"This evening. By the boat from Piraeus."

"Can you take me with you?"

"Okay. I'll make up some story for the new chaperone. But you've got to come right away. You called just in time. The kids are already on the bus."

"Thank God. Just have the bus stop in the Plaka, on Metropoleou Street. The Hotel Ermou. Room two-ten."

"Can you meet us at the door? I don't want to leave the kids alone."

"No. I can't. It's a matter of life and death. Just bring all the kids up to the room."

"The whole parade?"

"The whole parade."

"Okay. See you soon."

I hung up, and almost immediately the phone rang. I let it ring.

It seemed an eternity before the bus stopped in front of the hotel. It was so wide for the old street that it was parked half on the sidewalk. It was a pretty chancy way to escape notice, I thought, jamming my hat down over my curls and covering half my face with sunglasses, but it was all I had.

The whole parade could be heard mounting the stairs from the lobby. I shouldered my backpack.

"God!" said Debby when I opened the door. "You look like a midget private eye."

"Biffy and Diane," I muttered. "Stay one on each side of me while I check out and then walk fast right to the bus. Okay?"

"What's the deal?" said Biffy. "You hiding from the fuzz?"

"Actually, from a man" I said.

The familiar bell chime of giggles ran through the group of girls.

"Go!"

"It's a guy!"

Why hide?"

"I'll take him."

"Yeah. I need a date for homecoming."

In crocodile formation, with Debby in the lead and I and my escort in the middle, we descended the two flights of stairs and passed the lounge where slatted blinds were drawn against the sun. Emma and Jared were sitting there. In the dark little lobby, the courier leaned against the counter chatting with the proprietor, who idly tossed his worry beads. Standing between Biffy and Diane as I checked out and turned in my room key, I could smell Emma's perfume and hear her bracelets jingle.

"Shall we try the room again?" she asked.

"We should try to gain access in any way possible," said Jared. "She might be sick. Or injured. That could be our story."

The proprietor handed me my passport. "Let's go," I whispered. Between the two tall girls I walked rapidly out the front door. A few yards up the sidewalk, we boarded the bus. The courier swung herself in behind us. The doors hissed and closed, and the bus began to roll.

At the next corner, however, we were obliged to stop to allow a Greek priest to cross the street. Tall and grey bearded, he walked with a leisurely sacerdotal pace, like a one-man procession. On one arm, he carried a string bag of tomatoes and cucumbers.

In the side mirror, I saw Jared and Emma in the doorway of the hotel, looking after the bus. I slouched down in my seat. The bus began to move again.

Our progress through the city traffic was maddeningly slow, but once on the highway from Athens to Piraeus we made good time. The bus parked on the wharf where the excursion boats were tied up, and the courier gave me a quizzical look as she handed me my boat ticket.

The water of the harbor was calm in the grey and rose of the evening light. We were the last to board our ship, and the Greek sailors handed us aboard and drew up the gangplank behind us. The whistle sounded its deep farewell, the sailors pulled in the hawsers, and the water fizzed between the engines and the land as we backed out into the Saronic Gulf and slowly turned seaward. The concrete buildings of Piraeus fell away; and we saw in the distance against the mountain ranges of Attica the profiles of the Acropolis and it neighbor, the Hill of Lycobettus.

Debby jogged my elbow. "Are those your friends?" she asked.

In the foreground, a taxi had driven on to the wharf. Emma and Jared hurried to the boat landing, and I could see them gesturing and shouting at the official who had cast off the mooring lines. He shrugged and held up his hands. The distance between us widened, and they became almost invisible in the rapid southern twilight. I was tempted to wave.

CHAPTER SIXTEEN

We ate dolmades and pilaf and lamb in the ship's dining room, and afterwards we played poker with the students in our cabin over the thrumming engines. It was after midnight when the girls finally dispersed and I was able to tell Debby the story of my eventful day before we both fell into an exhausted sleep.

"I'll hate to see you go," Debby said the next morning over our breakfast of dried bread and pound cake and Greek coffee. "I worry about you. I'll be relieved to hear that you're all right and that this thing is over with. If I don't hear from you in, say, two days, shall I call the American consul? Or my Dad?"

"No thanks. I think I have relatives in Agios Titos. I'll be okay. I just had my fortune told by the ghost of a gypsy, and she told me so."

"God," said Debby. "You say the most amazing things."

The sky had lightened to grey-pink above the azure Aegean, and now the sunrise began, with the clouds on the horizon picking up the sunlight in great parallel bands of rose and fiery gold. Debby and I stared at each other. "Rhododactylos," she said. "The rosy-fingered dawn."

Soon the Island of Crete rose from the Icarian Sea, crowned by Mount Ida, and we steamed past the Venetian fort and breakwater of the city of Herakleion and docked among the kayaks and multicolored fishing boats. I took leave of the students on the ship to avoid the attention which they seemed to attract, especially from young men. After disembarking, I strode rapidly up the hill, past the outdoor tavernas and souvenir shops to the center of town.

A tourist policewoman directed me to the street corner from which the public bus was to depart to the south coast of Crete in an hour. Since the morning was still and fair and my shoulders ached from carrying the heavy pack so long and so far, I strolled back to the square in the middle of the city and sat down at a sidewalk café. I ordered a cup of Greek coffee and a pastry of nuts and honey and sat contentedly studying the Morosini Fountain with its lions of St. Mark and listening to the conversations in Greek and German and English around me. My fellow customers seemed to be mostly students and Classics teachers, down from England and northern Europe for Easter vacation. There were Englishwomen in hats and sturdy shoes, sunburned Scandinavians, and Germans in shorts and rucksacks.

Twenty minutes before my bus was due to leave, I wiped my fingers with the handkerchief that had been pressed into my hand by Maude Montero an aeon ago on the other side of the world. I shouldered the pack. Down the hill, on the Street of the Twenty-fifth of August, stood a Venetian loggia. I strolled past it and started down toward the harbor again. I noticed that the water, so cairn at dawn, had grown rough and patched with whitecaps. The day had grown warmer, and I felt a hot, dry wind at my back. It raised the dust in the street and fluttered the dresses that hung outside the shops that I passed. It flapped the sail of a caique that had just tied up at the harbor's edge and ruffled the hair of the tall, square-shouldered man whose back was to me as he secured the bow line. It blew back the trench coat of his companion, revealing that he wore a police revolver at his hip. As our eyes briefly met, I recognized Ben Porter, the Brightwater chief of police, whom I had barely eluded in the kitchen at Bluecove.

"Allo. Guten morgan. Kalemera," said the shopkeeper as I spun around and headed up the hill, keeping close to the wall.

"Hello, darling," said another as I nearly tripped over his steps. The bus was waiting at the corner. I boarded at the back and handed the ticket vendor one of the bills that Montero had given me. He gave me change and a ticket, and I sat on a bench beside a peasant woman in black. On her other side sat an old man in the Cretan dress of boots, voluminous trousers, and a lace head cloth.

The bus started up and wheezed through the square, avoiding, to my relief, the Street of the Twenty-fifth of August. Soon we left through a gate in one of the fortification walls and drove past the "tsimenta" works and ceramics factories on the outskirts. From time to time the bus stopped to take on a young woman with children or an old woman with a box of live chickens. The hot wind still blew, and dust and grit rattled against the side of the bus.

"It's the sirocco," said the old woman in Greek.

We headed inland and picked up speed. The mountain roads made hairpin turns over plunging chasms without guard rails. At one curve a motorbike blocked our way. The horn blared, the bus teetered over the precipice on two wheels, the cyclist held up his hand in a rude gesture and we continued upwards.

"It was a terrible thing last Friday," said the old woman. "A bus fell off the road. Many people were killed."

"Nai. Nai. Catastrophe. Catastrophe," the murmur went around the bus. A baby cried. The chickens squawked. I wondered if I had enough money to rent a car.

Soon the grade leveled off, and I wiped my hands on the knees of my slacks. We had come to the Plain of Massara, where for miles white stucco farmhouses stood among grapevines and fields of artichokes and tomatoes under plastic. There were groves of orange trees, and from the side of the road dark-eyed children waved branches of oranges. The leaves of the olive trees were silver, turned inside out by the sirocco.

The bus swayed around another curve, and we began the descent from the plain to the shore. Ahead of us glimmered the Libyan Sea, separating Europe from Africa. We passed a signpost with the name Agios Titos. Flowering mimosa trees lined the highway. I thought of the forsythia, first harbinger of the reluctant northern spring, far away in Michigan. The pack rested between my feet.

The bus turned another corner, and I looked down on the landscape which for so long had haunted my memory and my dreams. To my right the National Highway passed a high promontory from which the cliff fell away in a sheer drop to the sea below, where the waves, driven by the sirocco, pounded the rock face and threw sheets of spindrift into the air. Nearby, to take advantage of the view, was a little roadside café with little round tables set with fluttering linen tied down with plastic.

The main street was so narrow that the bus almost touched the houses on both sides. The white houses dazzled in the sun. Each had a red tile roof and a little courtyard, brilliant with geraniums. The bus stopped at the village plataea, and I swung myself down the step and stood blinking in the sun and wind, wondering what to do next.

At the corner of the square a sign pointed to the Xenia or inn, the Archaia or ruins, and the Museum. Tilting my body against the weight of the Brightwater Athena, I set off down the remembered street toward the museum. Roses bloomed in the forecourt, and as I approached the front door the lizards which had been sunning themselves on the doorstep fled away. Inside, it was cool and suddenly still. A slight man rose from behind a desk full of postcards and guidebooks. Against his white hair, his face was brown and deeply lined, but his dark eyes were young. They met mine and held them for a long time, until I felt suspended outside of time and space by his odd, fixed stare. Finally he spoke in Greek.

"Kalemera. Eimai Michael Stephenakis." This, then, was my mother's uncle. I looked away and responded in English. I was still fearful of revealing my identity and my errand until I had heard from Montero Courtney.

"Do you speak English?" I asked.

A flicker of disappointment crossed his face, but he smiled and answered, "Yes. I went to college and graduate school in the United States, so I enjoy using my English. Would you like to see the museum, Despoinis?"

"Yes. Please."

"Shall I check your backpack?"

"I'd ... I'd rather keep it with me. It has my passport and return ticket and all." He came out from behind the desk.

"As you wish. Would you like me to carry it for you?"

"No thanks. It's not heavy," I lied.

He guided me to the first gallery, where the sunlight fell in bright arches from the Venetian arcade. On the floor and in the cases were vases in every size, from pithoi large enough to hold Ali Baba to krateri, delicate as consommé cups. They were decorated with patterns of fish and plants — octopuses and dolphins, seaweed and flowers— in bold curves and spirals. "These are Minoan vases from about 1600 to 1400 B.C. They were excavated from the ruin just outside the village. Have you been there?"

"Not yet," I said. "I hope to go this afternoon."

"It's a small palace, perhaps the seaside villa of a Minoan nobleman. The sea came in closer in those days, before the earthquake which exploded the island of Santorini and destroyed so many Minoan palaces." He began to walk again. "Unfortunately, you are a few generations too late to see the treasure that was once the pride of this museum. This next gallery contains the personal collection of the Stephenakis family, which has been established here in Agios Titos since far before Venetian times. As far back as local records go."

"Your local records go back to Heroditus," I said, and he smiled again. We walked to the empty niche. "This," he said, "once held what is now called the Brightwater Athena."

I managed to look blank and inquiring.

"It is a model, probably by Phidias, of the Athena Polias, which once stood in the Parthenon, but was taken down in antiquity and melted down for the gold. The model somehow found its way to Constantinople, where it was seen and described in the fourth century by St. Ischyros of Rhodes. It was brought to Venice in the early fifteenth century by a collector fleeing the Turks, and it was later sold to a Venetian nobleman who brought it here to his villa on Crete. His heir in turn sold it to Nikos Stephanakis, an ancestor of mine, a prosperous merchant with a fleet of ships that traded all over the world. This museum was once his house."

"I see," I said.

"During the Turkish occupation the family grew less prosperous. They could no longer afford to live here, so they donated the house to the village as a museum. But to ensure that the family would have a source of wealth to fall back on in time of trouble, they kept the Athena, although they left it on display here. I am the fifth generation of my family to work as curator here."

"You are very fortunate," I said.

"Thank you. I agree." Then his eyes darkened. "More fortunate than my ill-fated grandfather."

"Was he curator when the Athena was lost?"

"She was stolen," he said. "An American came to Agios Titos in 1896. The Turks still governed Crete. He was an amateur archeologist and a complete fool. He bought a field in the back here, behind the gardens, from my family. He hired some men and began to dig in the most unprofessional manner possible. This of course was long before the other ruins were uncovered twenty years ago by the William Courtney expedition, and Evans had only acquired Knossos in 1894. But this man — Alfred Trapper was his name — had no interest in history or archeology as such. He had read about Scliemann's discoveries at Troy and he was after gold, pure and simple."

"Why do you think he chose Crete?" I interposed.

"Perhaps its remoteness. I think he thought that he could get away with his crime more easily here, and he was probably right. Cretans have always been independent, a law unto themselves. But after a month of gouging around the meadow like a savage, he had found no gold. So he broke into this museum at night. The next day he was gone, and so was the statue. He was shameless. He established it in his hideous mansion in a place called Brightwater in America and called it the Brightwater Athena. He took it only because it was gold." Michael's eyes were blazing. "If he had wanted to steal a work of art, the El Greco there in the next room was nearly as valuable. He did not care about the beauty of it or its history. Just the gold. He used it to secure financial backing and became a millionaire. However ..." He paused for a moment, and some of the anger died from his eyes. A chilly smile deepened the creases around his mouth. "One of the women of the village, the great grandmother of our caretaker, called down a malediction — a curse — on Alfred Trapper. She had been my grandmother's nurse and was the chief midwife of the village, and her maledictions, and her blessings, really worked. She could magic away tumors."

I felt the hair rise on the back of my neck.

"She said he and any of his descendants who kept the Athena would die by their own hands. Alfred Trapper jumped out of a skyscraper in New York after he was ruined in business. His son drank himself to death. I haven't kept up with the story of his child. It was a daughter, I think, with a Las Vegas showgirl that he married on his deathbed when the child was two or three years old. He was on leave from a mental hospital at the time.

I thought of pretty Emma and her beautiful clothes and her love of luxury. "Can't you get it back?" I asked at length. "Don't you have the provenance?"

"The political situation in Greece at the time made art theft easy. Look at Lord Elgin and the theft of the Acropolis marbles. They at least were lying outdoors unprotected. The Athena was well cared for in a village museum. But twenty years ago some American archeologists, William Courtney and his young nephew Monty — a nice kid, a student — and Robert Grey, who married my niece, came to excavate the Minoan palace outside the village. Young Monty, by the way, went on to publish a paper purporting to demonstrate beyond a doubt that the Athena was a nineteenth century fake. A brilliant piece of work and totally false, of course, but it took away the threat of further burglary for a while, or so we hoped."

We had reached his desk again, and he pulled out a chair for me before taking his own. I sat down with relief, shrugging off the pack and putting it between my feet.

"The expedition," Michael continued, "was financed by an American businessman who had made a hobby of archeology and had somehow heard about this village and the theft of the Athena. He was extraordinarily generous, but he exacted a promise from the family that caused some uncertainty at the time, but which I have come to think was for the best."

"What was that?"

"He wanted to buy the Athena if it were ever recovered. He would leave it here in Agios Titos, where he had planned to retire as in fact now he has. So we began to make a plan to bring her back." He paused and looked at me closely. "You must forgive me for the way I stared at you when you came in, but you look enough like my niece to have been her twin. But she would have been middle aged by now. She died young."

I half turned away. "I'm sorry" I said.

"They became interested in the story," he resumed, "and planned to bring her back. We gave what records we had to Robert Grey, who was a profound scholar. Unfortunately, he, too, died before his work was finished. Just this past year. He had had a weak heart since childhood. Rheumatic fever, I think."

"What happened to the records, the provenance?" I asked.

"Nobody seems to know. The archeologist, Montero Courtney..."

"I've heard of him," I said.

"He came here to talk to our priest, my brother, Robert's father-in-law, and said that Robert was working on the provenance but that it was incomplete. My brother gave him what little he had. Since then my brother, too, has died. So now the Athena and her papers and Mr. Badger's offer go to Robert and Sophie's daughter, a little girl — of course a grown woman by now — in the U.S."

Michael turned his searching look on me again, and, uneasy under his scrutiny, I stood and shouldered the pack. "Well, I wish you the best of luck," I said, "and thank you. It has been very interesting."

He walked with me to the front door which he opened. It framed the sunlit tableau of a Mercedes sedan with a woman at the wheel. It was Emma Trapper, and beside her in the passenger seat sat Jared Fender.

I spun around. "Is there another door, Mr. Stephenakis?"

"Straight out that way." I hurried the length of the hall and threw my weight against the heavy portal. It swung open, and I stood again in the sunlight. The Mercedes was there. I felt a sudden grip on both my arms from behind, and, before I could struggle, I was hustled into the car, which sped away. I found myself on the back seat next to Jared, staring at the golden hair of Emma Trapper.

CHAPTER SEVENTEEN

"Be calm, Athena. Remember, I am armed," Jared said.

"Where are you taking me?"

"Nowhere. It is only the statue we want."

Emma drove out of the village and up the steep road to the cliff over the sea. At the roadside café she shifted into low with a lurch and a grinding of gears and crawled almost to the edge of the cliff, from which the car rolled back slightly from the upward incline and ground again to a stop.

"Your brakes are gone," I said.

"How perceptive of you to notice," he replied. I felt the gun in my side.

"You wouldn't dare shoot me in front of all these people," I said.

"But there is nobody here." He was right. Because of the wind, the café was deserted.

I reached for the strap of my pack, but he wrested it from me with a strong hand. Emma opened the door of the back seat, and he stepped out, turning to help me as if this were a normal social occasion. I walked between my captors to the place where a tablecloth fluttered beneath the tossing branches of a plane tree. Jared pulled out a chair for me, and Emma sat on my other side. A boy in a white coat came out, and Jared ordered a bottle of retsina. When it came, he poured it out into three little glasses.

"You understand your position," he said. "You might as well relax and enjoy your wine. Then you will tell us where to find your father's papers, the provenance of the Athena."

"I don't know where they are."

"You lie. But it doesn't matter. We have the monument, and it is valuable enough as it is." He refilled my glass.

"I'm hungry," I said, and he signaled the waiter.

"Yesplizz?"

"Bread and cheese and olives for the young lady, please."

"Thankyouveddymuch."

"If you help us," Jared resumed, "we will share part of the fortune with you. If not, there will be a tragic accident."

"What are you going to do with me?" The waiter brought bread in a plastic basket and a square of feta cheese surrounded by shining black olives. I swallowed with great difficulty, although I remember now that the bread was good.

"In trying to escape us, you will accidentally drive over the cliff when the brakes of our rented Mercedes fail, as I have arranged. We Fenders are good car mechanics."

I looked at the profile of the Mercedes, etched against the sky, above the abyss. Emma refilled her glass. "Did you kill my father?" I asked.

"There was no need," Jared said. "That night I came to see him, to persuade him to give us the provenance of the monument that is rightfully ours. But I was too late. I searched the house, but you had already taken the papers"

"So it was you." I was aware of a sense of the imminent solution to many mysteries as well as the danger to my life, and my mind was alert. "Why do you keep saying that it is yours when Alfred Trapper left it to Emma?" Their eyes met, and that odd spark that I had noticed at the Castle arced between them again.

"What's mine is Jared's," Emma said. "We have been married for twenty years."

"What?"

"Judge Courtney married us secretly before Victor was born. Ostensibly it was for Victor's sake — those things mattered in those days, at least in places like Brightwater. But we both wanted it, and I think that he wanted to be sure that Monty, who was the overprotective bossy gentleman even then, wouldn't try to make an honest woman of me. As it was, they took Victor off our hands, which at the time was the best thing for everybody. Although ... sometimes...well, that's over and done with."

"Then Montero isn't Victor's biological father?"

"Mr. sweetness and light? God no!" Her laughter pealed. "He's hardly even touched me, in all these years. It was Jared, of course."

"And he never knew you were married?"

"Nobody did, except for the three of us and the judge's old secretary, who died within the year. Not even old Maude."

"But why?"

Emma shrugged. "Why not? The Judge was a lot like his son Monty. Always interfering in other people's lives, righting other people's wrongs. Remember that this was twenty years ago, and the Judge and William Courtney, who, by the way, is Jared's father, lovely place Brightwater, anyway, they wanted to send him to a good boarding school off in the wilds of the mid-west to make sure he developed his potential."

"Which was in some jeopardy after I shot my stepfather when I found him in bed with my grandmother," Jared said with that wince of a smile. I shivered, thinking of Silas Fender.

"Then why all the charade in Brightwater?" I asked. "Why the official engagement?"

"You ask too many questions," Jared responded.

"Wait, darling." said Emma. "I think she has a right to know. After all, you both did toy with her affections." Their gaze met again. I felt my color rise. Emma turned her large eyes to me. The pupils were like pinpricks. "Monty had this thing, that he owed me something for stealing my only inheritance. As of course he did. With the official engagement, he had settled on me one of those trusts from the Bluecove estate, enough to keep me in genteel poverty for life. Of course, the truth would have come out of the sealed county records when he went to get a license, but by then Jared, I, the trust, and the Athena would have been long gone. In fact, it was his less than ardent wooing that tipped us off to the fact that he was finally going to do this. That and your meeting with Jared in New York."

"Do you remember that day, my dear?" said Jared. "What an extraordinary coincidence. You see, when the sad news of Sophie's accident came to Monty years ago, he told me that you and Robert had also been killed. I believed him, of course. Sweetness and light was also truth and integrity. The Fenders lived in a morass of lies and intrigue, not the Courtney's. Strange, isn't it, that I believed him? Then I met you, and everything changed. Emma began to watch Monty more closely. Sharing the museum telephone, it wasn't hard to keep track of him. Even Miss Adams joined in the spying on him and Gus." Jared gave a bitter laugh. "When he went to Michigan, I followed him. You see, Montero Courtney had taken everything. Everything in my life that had any meaning for me. My place as William Courtney's boy at Bluecove. The heart of the girl that I had been sleeping with since we were hardly more than children ..."

"Jared. No. Never." Crystal tears began to stream down Emma's alabaster cheeks.

"But I wanted it all back. I wanted Emma. I wanted her fortune, the little statue that he first discredited and then stole. I even wanted you for a moment, because I could see that he loved you as he had never loved anyone. So. Where are the papers?"

"I don't know. Truly, I don't know."

"Then we have no more use for you," he said. The table rocked as he stood up. He held his right hand in his coat pocket. It seemed as if the earth had stopped in its rotation and we were all frozen in space. "Just walk calmly," he said, "toward the car. It won't take a minute."

I refused to move. He came closer. I glanced at the door of the café. The proprietor and waiter were inside. Emma had risen and stood at my other side. Behind Jared I saw a car in the distance, beginning to climb up the curving hill. Jared moved closer, and I sidestepped. He jerked the revolver out of his pocket, and I raised my hands in the air.

The car, a miniature marked police car, spun into the driveway in a shower of gravel, and Montero and Ben Porter were there with a uniformed Greek policeman.

I was suddenly jerked, not by Jared but by Emma, sideways into the Mercedes, which she locked and started up, gunning the engine, heading toward the precipice. There was an explosion of gunfire. As I stared, Jared threw himself onto the hood of the car, as if to stop her. She jerked into reverse with a shrieking of gears, but it was too late. Jared began to fall backwards. Montero bolted forward and caught his arm, and for a minute the two men hung suspended at the edge. Immediately Ben Porter was at Montero's side, but Jared slipped through his grasp and was gone, leaving his cousin still leaning over the sea, reaching out.

Emma careened backwards toward the highway. A car swerved around us with a screaming of brakes and a rude gesture from the driver. She plunged forward up the hill, her eyes glazed, her mouth set in a strange grin. The car rocked crazily. The gunshots had destroyed the tires. At the top of the hill she swerved off the road, speeding straight to the sea. I reached over, turned off the ignition, and yanked out the key. Miraculously, the car bottomed on a rock and crashed to a stop, the front wheels almost over the edge. Emma turned her dazed face to me, and I slapped her, so that her head snapped against the headrest. Her eyes cleared.

"I'm going to him," she said. "And you're coming with me. Both Athenas."

"No," I said. "Listen. There's a curse on the Athena. Keep her and you'll be a suicide. Like your father and grandfather. Give her back and you'll live."

"For what?"

"For Montero."

"I hate him."

"For Victor."

Over her shoulder, I saw Ben at her window. I reached across her and unlocked her door, which he yanked open. Her hand shot out and put the car in neutral. The front wheels went over the rock. I leapt out into the arms of Montero, but I pushed him aside and flung open the back door of the car and grasped the strap of the pack, feeling my arm wrenched out of its socket as the car gained momentum and the front tilted down the promontory.

It went end over end as if in slow motion down the rock face, stopped for a moment on a ledge, where it burst into flames. Black smoke streamed toward us in the salt wind before the car somersaulted into the water and the surf boiled over it.

Montero held me until I stopped shaking. "Thank God," he kept saying. "Thank God."

"She's passed out," Ben said.

"I have not!" I protested, but then I saw that Ben was leaning over Emma, who lay on the ground. The Greek policeman spoke into his cell phone, and then said something in Greek to Montero.

"They got Jared," he said to Ben.

In the distance, a siren wailed. Emma stirred and moaned.

"Is he alive?" Ben asked.

"Barely. I don't think he is going to stand trial."

"Stand trial?" I asked. "For what?"

"For murder."

"Murder? Who?"

"Si Fender," said Ben.

"The snake?"

"No. That could have been an accident," said Montero. "Si was shot by Jared's gun which was then put into his own hand so that it would look like suicide."

I stared at him speechless. I reached down for the backpack, but the gesture brought an explosion of pain in my shoulder, and I felt myself caught again as I fell.

CHAPTER EIGHTEEN

When I recovered consciousness, I was in a bed in the small village hospital, and my right shoulder was tightly taped. I heard the sound of a woman weeping, and turning my head on my pillow I saw Emma on the bed next to me, her face wet with tears. Montero sat between us, and Ben Porter, still in his trench coat, stood at Emma's other side.

"He didn't make it. I'm sorry, Emma," he was saying. "As soon as you are up to it, you'll have to come down to the police station and answer some questions. You have the right to remain silent..."

"Oh shut up, Ben," Emma said groggily. "Go away. I want to talk to Monty. Alone."

I closed my eyes and turned my face back to the wall.

"It's all right, Ben," said Montero.

"I'll be right outside the door," said the detective, and I heard his footsteps retreat.

"You know that Jared and I were married by your father, that summer that you were away," Emma said.

"No. I never knew."

"Do you mind?" she said, very low. There was no answer. "Always the gentleman," she said bitterly at length. "You never loved me. A woman knows these things. You were a nice kid and a good friend, but there was never any... you know I never loved you."

"I wouldn't have asked you to."

"You would have condemned me to a life of living hell, a lie, a fantasy, a false marriage, when I had a real one? With Jared."

"Emmy."

"All in the name of your idea of morality. Just like the whole phony world of Bluecove. All books. All playacting. Costume's and dress up. The theater. Charades at Christmas. All you Courtney's know how to do is pretend. All you bright beautiful people, up there in the light, playing games. Nobody actually ever living. Well, what Jared and I had was real. The Fenderbog was down there in the dark, all full of wrecked cars and mud and mold and people screwing their own in-laws. No wonder Jared was precocious. But it was real. No one screws anybody at Bluecove." Her sobs became shaky laughter. "Sorry, Monty. Nothing personal. You did kiss me once or twice. It was kind of fun."

"Please, Emmy."

"Oh, I hate you. Go away. I hate Brightwater. And everybody in it. I never want to see it again. Or you. I wish your little friend had never stopped me." She gave a shuddering sigh, and then her weeping stopped abruptly. There was a silence before, in a steady voice, she said, "Victor."

"Victor?"

"I'm going to let you have that goddammed statue — no, don't interrupt me. I know. I have no right to it anyway, and I'm sure that you'll get the Grey papers as soon as that poor creature comes to. But she gave me an idea. I want to do this of my own accord. I want to present it officially and above board, to the village. Righting old wrongs. The whole bit. After all, it was my grandfather who stole it and bequeathed it to me. But first I want to make a deal with you. A trade."

"A trade?"

"The Athena for Victor."

"I don't understand."

"He's the heir to the Manor and Jared's gallery. Jared made the will years ago, leaving a generous bit of capital to me as well. By the way, you can have your silly trust back. If they don't send me to jail, I'll have plenty. Jared was pretty rich, you know. He just felt deprived. Nothing was ever enough. He always needed more. More fame. More money. More women. That's why we never announced our marriage. He never thought we had enough to start our life together, so I was just left hanging around Brightwater, drinking and doping the time away.

"He always came back to you."

"Oh I know. I never expected him to be faithful any more than he expected it of me. What we had was more than that. But now, for the first time in my life I'm free." There was a silence before she continued. "You know something funny? Jared took more than my virginity all those years ago in the spare room at the Castle."

"Emma. Please."

"No. Listen to me. For once. I know you don't think I'm smart. And I'm not, not the way you and Athena are. But there are things I know, and I know that Jared in that awful neediness took something from both you and me. He took away most of me. Myself. That's why I don't feel as bad as I thought I would, now that it's all over. And he took some part of you as well. It's as if he was so bad that you had to be too good. Solving all the problems of everyone. But now I'm free. I never want to go back to Brightwater again. And I don't want Victor growing up like his father, all twisted up because he was deprived of his real place."

"He has a place at Bluecove as well. And I can't choose for him. He has to do that himself."

"You're making progress already, Monty darling." As her emotion subsided, her voice was returning to her normal drawl. "Even a week ago you would have chosen for him. Just like your father, Judge God Courtney, running everyone else's life." She gave another shuddering sigh, and I heard her sit up and set her feet on the floor. "So that's the end of it, Monty. I'll ring the nurse and get dressed. There's nothing wrong with me that a good stiff drink won't fix. And if Ben and those enchanting Greek cops don't send me to jail I'm going to check myself into rehab back in the states and then put my whole past in that hell hole of a dead end behind me forever. You'll never see or hear from me again. Well. Let me know when your little friend comes out of it. I think she deserves to be there for the restoration. She saved my life, I guess, as well as your precious statue. If she has any sense she'll also get the hell out of Brightwater forever."

"I'll stay here with her until I know she's all right."

"Well, I'll be at the police station with Ben."

"Emmy."

"Yes, Monty?"

"I won't bother you anymore, but I need to know."

"What, darling?"

"Would you have done it? Would you have killed her, if we hadn't come?"

"I ... Remember I had just seen Jared ... I blacked out. It has happened a few times recently. I had taken some stuff to steady my nerves as well as all that wine. All I remember is that she slugged me. I might have. I don't know. I wanted to kill myself as well. You see why I have to go away. Forever."

"Yes. I see."

The nurse bustled in and pulled shut the curtain, and Montero stepped out to the corridor. "Just one minute, Kyrie," she said. I heard her help Emma get dressed and restored to the capable custody of Ben Porter. Then she came to my side of the curtain and pulled down my hospital nightgown and applied a stethoscope so cold that my eyes flew open and I gasped. "There. That's better. More asleep than unconscious. The painkiller, you know. And so tired. There we are, Despoinis."

She helped me on with my clothes and then opened the door. Montero looked gaunt and exhausted, and there were dark shadows under his eyes. But when he saw me, his smile seemed to light the room. He took my two hands in his, and his eyes unexpected filled with tears. He was unable to speak.

"I'm sorry about Jared," I said. "Your evil twin."

He cleared his throat and waited for his voice to be steady. "Well, they wanted him for the murder of Si Fender. I guess he finally did it. But he would have hated prison. I ... I couldn't bring myself to call Veronica. I'll tell her in person when we get back. It's the end of an old, sad story."

I realized that Silas might well have ended his own life saving me, but I said nothing. What difference would it make now? "What about the snake?" I asked.

"The snake went for a rat. Lovely place, the Fender Manor. Someone called 911, maybe Si, or Veronica, and Ben was there right away and shot the snake. The miracle is that you got away. I still can't believe you gave them the slip. And me as well. In Athens. Ben and I were on the flight right after yours. But we did succeed, after all. Thanks to you. And as soon as the Athena is in her place, I am going to take you safe home."

"What home, Monty?" I said softly. "I have no home."

Before he could respond, the nurse appeared. "Your uncle is here," she said. "After your visit is finished, the doctor will check you out."

"So he guessed," I said to Montero, who smiled as Michael Stephenakis came to the door. "I'm sorry I tried to fool you," I said as he bent ceremoniously to kiss my cheek.

"Not for long," he answered. "I knew you had to be Sophie's child, especially since I was expecting Monty any day. That's why I called the police the minute you left."

"Where do we go from here?" I asked, looking from one to the other.

"Bart Badger is waiting to hear from me," Montero said. "If it's all right with you, and if Ben agrees, since he has her in custody, I'll call Bart from here while they're checking you out. I'd like to have Emma return the statue to the museum as she wished before Ben takes her back to Brightwater."

"Of course," I said. "But, just out of curiosity, why?"

"I don't know. It's just a gesture, since Bart means to display it there anyway. For her sake, somehow."

"It is a wise gesture," said Michael. "It should lift the malediction. I will tell you about it later, Monty."

"Then we'll go to Bart's house, or villa —"

"Or palace," smiled Michael.

"And finally transact this sale. Ned O'Neill flew in this morning. He may be there already." His quick smile lit up my heart. "And you, my dear, will be a millionaire." The nurse came in with the young doctor, and Montero pressed my hand before he drew out his cell phone and left with my Uncle Michael.

When we arrived at the police station, the waiter from the roadside café was telling what he had witnessed, with both drama and accuracy. The police questioned us and wrote in their record books; and Emma was released to the custody of Ben Porter. They were to be driven by the local police, with Jared's coffin, to Herakleion for the next flight back to the United States.

Montero carried the backpack out into the sunlight, and we walked in a group to the Plataea. Montero laid the pack on the table, and I opened it and lifted out the Athena, heavy and shining, and handed it to Emma.

There was a stir throughout the Plataea. Villagers gathered from the surrounding tables. Old men crossed the square from the caffeneion. They formed an impromptu procession behind us as Michael gravely led Emma into the cool shadows of the museum. We stopped at the niche, and Emma stood holding the Agois Titos Athena for a minute before she handed it to Montero, who placed it back where it belonged.

As we left the building, Michael walked beside Emma, speaking in a low voice. "Did you know about the malediction?"

"They used to talk about the Trapper curse, when I was a little girl. Because of my father and grandfather," she said.

"Well, it is finished now," he said. He shook her hand. "Thank you, Kyria Fender."

She turned blindly away, shook hands wordlessly with Montero and then with me, as if in a trance, and Ben led her off to the police car which was parked in front of an old hearse. The two vehicles moved away up the mountainside and were soon lost to sight. As the hearse disappeared around the curve, I thought of Jared's blighted promise, his strange sensitivity and insight, and Emma's words about Victor. I began to form a plan to help the son of the troubled and wicked man who had such rare knowledge of the human heart.

Michael and Montero returned to the square and ordered wine and bread and platters of mezes, a celebration for all who wished to join us. Michael could not stop smiling, and his joy was reflected in the dark eyes and sunburned faces around us. The story was repeated again and again of the American archeologists and their adventure of bringing home the lost Athena and of their own Athena, the American granddaughter of their old priest, whom the new priest, now old himself, had worked under faithfully for years.

"And when are you coming back to resume the excavation?" Michael asked Montero. "It has been waiting for you all these years."

"We're hoping for next summer, now that Will is retiring from teaching. But we haven't got the funding yet," Montero said.

"Don't be silly," I started to say, but before he could respond, the old foreman tapped his arm, and soon the two were absorbed in reminiscences while the priest drew me to his side and began to talk of my grandparents.

The wind had dropped in the late afternoon and the air was still and warm, filled with the ringing of the cicadas and the songs of birds which had been stilled by the sun of midday. Montero took my hand and drew me aside.

"Would you come for a walk with me?" he asked. "And get away from all these nice people? Please."

We took a path out of the village up toward the visionary mountains, through a splendor of wildflowers. As we mounted the slope, wild orchids and white narcissus and lavender anemones gave way to fields of daisies and red poppies. The air from the sea was heavy with the fragrance of orange and lemon blossoms.

"Tell me everything," I said. "First, about your book that proved the Athena was a fake."

"Robert and I cooked that up that summer when I was still a student. To give him time. And keep Jared off our trail. You and I will have to write another."

"Courtney and Grey," I said, liking the sound. "Did Gus take the key to the case?"

"Of course."

"How did Jared and Emma trace me to the Hotel Ermou?"

"They knew of it before. I always stay there when I am in Athens."

"What happened after I left Bluecove?"

"They caught Victor and me, as we had intended, so that you could get away. They took us back to the police station, but of course we had no stolen property with us. I told Ben about the original theft. Then he was called to the Manor because of a grisly accident."

"I knew about that," I said.

We had reached a tiny deserted Byzantine chapel, and we sank down among the wildflowers, leaning our backs against the warm stone. Around us, the crickets sang of all antiquity, and from a nearby orange grove the nightingale began to pour out its immemorial music.

I drew a breath, which came out as a sort of shaky sigh, and steadied myself with a quick bite to my lower lip. "So that's it. It's all over. Except the actual sale, of course. I'm sorry I didn't give you the papers right away. When I left Michigan, it was to bring them to you; but then everything seemed so strange and sort of sinister and I felt like such an outsider, and you and Emma ... " I was obliged to clamp my teeth on my lip again, and I stared out over the white village to the blue sea and the blue horizon.

"Athena, my dear."

"Yes?"

"You understand about Emma, don't you?"

Watching the flight of a seabird, I could not bear to look at him, but I couldn't lie to him either. "I was awake when she was talking to you. In the hospital."

"I had always thought of it as my obligation, because we were taking all she had. I didn't know that Jared was probably supporting her, maybe even rather handsomely. They both were always talking about how poverty stricken she was."

"I noticed that. I am beginning to think it was a scam."

"But how were Robert and I to know? We planned this twenty years ago, but ... I had always hoped that it would not come to my actually having to marry her. But when Jared came back, an official engagement at least seemed the only way to keep her safe from Jared and you safe from her. She acts sweet enough when sober, but she can be dangerous... "

"I know. Miss Adams thinks she was poisoned by Emma."

"It's quite feasible. God knows, Emma had been poisoning herself for long enough. I knew, of course, that she and Jared were Victor's parents, but I never guessed that they were married. Jared was always so . . . Well. Then you came back to me. And I knew at once that I loved you. Remember, at the hospital, when you looked at me with those eyes and said it was weird?"

Turning my gaze away from the sea I felt as if I would sink into the deeper blue of his eyes. His smile flashed. "And I fell in love with you then and there. To be honest, I had never even liked Emma that much. I was in agony. And then, my poor love, you had just lost Robert." He put his arm around me, gently, because of my taped shoulder and drew me to his side. "Athena. I'm not very good at this. Now that you have finally come into your inheritance, what had you planned to do next?"

"I had planned to go back to Ann Arbor, to my old life," I said. "That's why I was all packed." With his other hand he cradled my chin and stroked my cheek and then bent and kissed my mouth, for a long time. I touched his cheek and the hollow of his temple in wonder. It didn't seem possible that after all the terror and danger, the flight and pursuit, the pain and fatigue, that this could be real. He kissed me again and soon I was returning his kisses and all my pain and tiredness were gone.

"Athena, will you marry me?" he said later. We were both breathing hard. "I should have asked you last winter when you first appeared like a little ghost in your father's house." I studied his face, my hand to his rough cheek. I felt as if my bones were melting. "If you don't want to," he said, "I'll love you forever anyway and follow you to Ann Arbor and take good care of you and never let you out of my life again."

"You would do that? Leave Brightwater? And Bluecove?"

"My only home is with you. Wherever you are." He began to kiss me again, and the fragrance of crushed wildflowers rose around us. Our bodies had begun to show a will of their own.

"Yes," I whispered," and again, "Oh, yes."

"I forgot about your injury," he said later, for his head was resting on my ace bandage.

"So did I," I smiled.

"Here." He re-fastened enough buttons and zippers to make us both respectable and re-arranged us so that I rested against him, and we drowsed among the flowers as the Greek sun declined.

Soon I raised my head from his shoulder and propped myself on my good arm, looking down at him. "I think you're very good at this," I whispered, and we both smiled.

"We should go back down," he said later.

"And will you take me back to Bluecove?" I asked. "It will be home to both of us."

"It won't be easy for you. The past is always present in Brightwater."

"But isn't that the business of the archeologist? The past? Besides, I'm pretty tough."

"I know you are," he said and drew me to him again.

CHAPTER NINETEEN

As we approached the village, I relinquished his hand and we stood still on the hillside. "Do you mind, is it all right if we don't tell anyone for a little while? This is all so new. It would be nice if it were just between us while I'm getting used to it."

"Of course, my pet." I stretched up to kiss him, wondering if I could ever get used to this happiness. "And, besides, I don't want to look like a fortune hunter."

My face must have changed, for he put his arms around me and pressed me to his chest. "I'm sorry," he said. "I know it doesn't seem funny to you."

"I suppose I will get used to it someday. Come on. Let's go and see Ned and Mr. Badger and get this over with."

Mr. Badger's villa stood on an outcropping of rock commanding a view of the village on one side and the sea on the other. It was built of white stucco and terra cotta in the local fashion but it was the size of a small village in itself.

"Have you been here before?" I asked as we mounted the staircase to the front door, where a servant ushered us into an atrium. The space included a fountain and splashing pool as well as several statues, the largest, a marble athlete attributed to Scopas, one of the best surviving from antiquity. I tried not to gape.

"Several times. Wait until you see the swimming pool."

There was a sound of footsteps along the arcade, and a slender grey-haired man approached us, extending his hand. I had expected a stereotypical business man, but he looked more like a scholar or an old monk, shy and bespectacled, with a strong resemblance to his daughter.

"Miss Grey? Bart Badger. This is certainly a pleasure. And Monty. Welcome. Mr. O'Neill is waiting for us."

Mr. O'Neill, looking cool and jaunty in white linen shirt and slacks and Greek sandals, rose from the library table as we entered the book-lined room. We sat down and he snapped open his briefcase and began to pass around an assortment of papers. To this day I scarcely remember what transpired, for my memory is so dominated by the moment when I held before my dazzled eyes a transaction informing me that five million dollars had been deposited in accounts opened for me by Mr. O'Neill in banks in Brightwater and Michigan. "Only temporarily, of course," he assured me. "As soon as we return to the States I would be happy to help you in any way to invest your inheritance as you wish."

"Thank you, Ned," was all I could say.

"And thank you, Miss Grey," Bartholomew Badger said. "I have looked forward to this day for many years."

"Athena. Please," I said.

"Athena." His smile warmed his myopic eyes. "And now my driver is bringing the car around. I had planned to take Mr. O'Neill down to Matala so that he can see something of the island before we take Debbie and her fifteen girls out to dinner. We'll be back in time to fly in my own jet to Brightwater Airpark, arriving tomorrow morning. We hope that you can both fly with us."

"Thank you," Montero said. "That way, with no connections to make to Athens then to Boston, we should get home before Ben and Emma. I would like to speak to Jared's family privately before they hear from the police or the media."

"I understand," Mr. Badger said. "We all regret this needless tragedy." He turned to me again. "You are welcome to come to Matala, Athena, but after all you have been through, you might prefer to dine here with Monty. Marco and Eleutheria will make you comfortable."

My first day as a millionaire was looking promising. I did not dare catch Montero's eye. "If you'd like to swim," Mr. Badger continued, "there are extra bathing suits in the guest suite. Debby often brings young friends with her, so we keep a supply of new ones on hand."

"Thank you. That would be lovely. Although we'll miss you at dinner," I lied.

"But we'll have time to visit during the flight tonight. Come. I'll show you your room."

I picked up my pack, nearly falling over sideways with the habit of compensating for the weight of the Athena. Montero caught me with an arm around my waist and a quick hug. "I'll meet you at the pool in a few minutes," he said, and I felt a ripple of excitement so intense that it frightened me.

"This is our housekeeper, Eleutheria," Mr. Badger said when we met a middle-aged woman at the top of the staircase. "Despoinis Grey will be eating dinner with Kyrios Courtney and flying back with us tonight." Eleutheria bent her head with a dignified acknowledgement of my greeting and took my pack away.

The room was enormous, but airy and sparsely furnished in the Greek fashion. Three French windows opened to a balcony over the terrace and swimming pool. As I opened one of them and stepped out, Eleutheria returned. "I have drawn a bath, Despoinis. If you wish to swim afterwards there are bathing suits in the wardrobe." Her eyes swept over me with a glimmer of humor. "The only one small enough for you, I am afraid, is very small, but Despoinis Badger has left some..." her hands gestured a beach cover-up.

"Eucharisto," I smiled.

"Parakalo." She returned the smile. The young doctor had said that that my dislocated shoulder was mending well and that I could remove the ace bandage as long as I avoided any more heavy lifting.

Eleutheria helped me to unwrap it before she slipped silently away down the long corridor. I basked in the tub in a sensual daze, remembering the afternoon, looking forward to the evening, before I wrapped myself in a giant towel and searched the armoire for a bathing suit. Eleutheria was right. The only one in my size was a fiendishly becoming bikini. I slipped Debby's shift of white cotton and Greek embroidery over my skin and fastened my sandals. I needed no make-up. My lips and cheeks were already flushed, and my eyes were dark and lustrous.

Montero and I met at the archway from the atrium to the terrace, smiling like two children freed from parental supervision.

He was wearing a Greek shirt over bathing trunks, and I thought I had never seen anything as beautiful as his long elegant legs.

I turned, and he drew me to him and kissed the back of my neck. "Shall we swim?" I whispered at length.

"I suppose so," he smiled and released me. "The servants are everywhere." I had to slip into the pool to cool off. We swam lazily to the deep end, and soon our legs were tangling. Out of the corner of my eye, I saw the butler glide on to the terrace carrying a tray. "Marco!" I whispered against Montero's lips, and we started apart so quickly that it is lucky we didn't drown. We were still out of breath when we reached the shallow end and pulled ourselves out of the water.

Marco had set the table with a tray holding a bottle of champagne in a silver ice bucket and plates of mezes — black olives and white cheese, tiny savory pastries, stuffed grape leaves and the thin-skinned tomatoes of Greece, the best in the world.

"I'll change quickly," I said, for the swift twilight was falling. "You won't go away?"

"Never. Not ever".

Eleutheria had ironed and laid out the only dress I had packed for my escape from Brightwater, the English flowered print that I had last worn on the night of Emma's dinner party. I felt a little chill as I buttoned it, wondering if Montero and I would ever fully exorcize Jared's ghost. But a glance at the night-backed window showed me a radiant young woman, wholly changed from the lonely waif of that evening which now seemed so long ago and far away.

Montero was leaning on the balustrade looking out at the sea as the great southern stars began to light like lamps. He pulled me to him until I said, "Marco," and we separated, laughing.

He moved to the table. "Champagne?"

"Lovely."

We touched glasses, newly aware of the solemnity of the moment. Then for a while we stood together watching the lights of a cruise ship as it glided into the harbor. A full moon was rising, laying a silver track upon the sea. "Do you suppose," I said at last, "that we'll still be saying 'Marco' when the grandchildren catch us making out at Bluecove?"

"Bluecove," he said. "After all these years. I still can't believe my luck. You at Bluecove. All that I love in the world."

"And yet you would have followed me to Ann Arbor," I said, and the moonlight revealed the quick smile that had grown so dear to me.

"Well, I hadn't given up hope of luring you back eventually," he admitted. "Did you really mean it? Will you say it again? That you'll marry me?"

"Of course." I burrowed my head into his chest.

"I haven't got a ring or anything at the moment..."

"I hate engagements," I blurted out, and I felt a chill, as when a shadow crosses the sun. "Let's just get married plain."

"My little lamb." He caressed my curls. "Of course." He led me back to the table, where Marco had lit four candles. "Remember that night in Greektown? I wanted to marry you then and there."

"I was just about to say that. It's funny. The money should mean a lot to me, but it doesn't. Given a choice, I'd rather have you."

"You won't be given a choice. You'll always have me."

Marco removed the first course and brought in plates of little grilled birds and pilaf and side dishes of the tender Cretan artichokes, spread open like water lilies on a pond of avgolemono. He refilled our champagne glasses.

"As my trustee as well as my fiancé," I said, "will you help me re-open the excavation at Agios Titios?"

"Only if you'll hire me," he smiled.

"Of course. And William."

"He will love it." His face suddenly grew grave, the eyes dark and remote, giving him that haunting resemblance to Jared. "That reminds me. I have to tell Will about Jared. And Veronica, too."

"I'm sure Will would rather tell her himself."

"No. I will do it. I can't dodge the responsibility."

"But," I started to object, but his face had grown hard. I recognized the overprotectiveness that I had remarked before, but I gave a shrug of my mental shoulders. It was the dark side of the quality that had first attracted me to him, his almost archaic sense of obligation and honor. "Then I'll go with you, of course."

"No. That's out of the question," he said. I stared at him between the wavering candle flames.

"What do you mean it's out of the question?"

"I can't let you go into that..." he shook his head. "No. I'll go to the Fender Manor alone. You can wait for me at Bluecove."

"I will not."

"What do you mean, Athena?" He had grown so pale that the freckles caused by the Greek sun stood out on his nose and cheekbones.

"I mean that I will go to the Fender manor with you and your Uncle William to tell Mrs. Fender about Jared."

"I won't have it. As your trustee, soon your husband... "

It seemed as if an abyss had opened between us and I hung over it, about to fall. "Yes?" I said. I hoped he wouldn't answer.

"I can't allow it, Athena."

The words seemed to echo and re-echo in my heart, as if a door had opened into some vast cave from which blew a cold draft, a chilling emanation from my childhood under the domination of my remote and lonely father, whom I had loved so desperately. Something in my face seemed to frighten him, for he grew even whiter and leaned against the back of his chair, taking a deep breath.

"You know nothing about that place, those people," he said.

"How do you know that?" I asked with deadly calm.

"I just know. You couldn't. You're an innocent lamb. I could no more let you go there than send you into — any kind of — you simply couldn't know."

"I am not an innocent lamb." I had never so clearly understood the metaphor of boiling blood. I was so angry that I heard a roaring in my ears, and I made an effort to keep my voice low and level. "I know as much as I need to know about the Fender family and maybe more than you do."

"Don't be absurd."

"Don't. Call. Me. Absurd."

"But you have to be from Brightwater ..."

"And I'm not. So it comes to this. No matter what, I am still an outsider, the foreigner in your world."

"Yes. It can't be helped."

"Montero. There's something you have to understand before we go any further. You can't live my life for me. I have to be free to make my own mistakes and pay the consequences of those mistakes. I mean to go to Fender manor. I am also going to ask Mr. O'Neill to help me establish a trust fund for Victor so that when he inherits it, as he will — you can't do anything about it — when he inherits it he will be able to restore it to what it once was."

"I won't allow it." He stood up. I did, too, on the other side of the abyss. "You know nothing of these people, and I do. Athena, you are a sweet and innocent girl. The Fenders have ruined our lives. They ruined William's. They ruined mine ..."

"Nobody made you go after Emma. You did it yourself."

"I had to."

"Why?"

He turned away, thrusting his hands down into his trouser pockets. "What did you mean when you said 'before we go any further'?" he asked at length.

"Montero. I can't ...love isn't keeping someone out of all possible harm."

"Of course it is." His eyes were huge and dark. From the front of the house there was the sound of the door shutting and voices echoing down the marble of the atrium.

"Don't you know that old saying," I said softly, in despair, "'To love someone is to set her free'?"

"But not to her own destruction. Freedom isn't neglect."

"But neglect doesn't apply to us. You're not my father. I had a father and he died."

"I'm soon to be your husband. I have a duty, an obligation, no matter what my feelings are."

"What feelings? What do you mean? That you don't love me anymore?"

"You said it. I didn't. But that shouldn't change anything. I will stay with you no matter what. I said I would and I will."

"As you did with Emma?"

"Yes," he said defiantly.

"Then you really will have to set me free. I could never be trapped in such an arrangement."

"Do you mean you won't marry me?"

"I can't. Don't you understand?"

He turned away again. His voice was low and steady. "I knew it would come to this. I knew that Emma and Jared would somehow come between us. And now the Fenders have reached out again and completed their destruction of ... your life, too, as well as mine."

"Only if we let them."

"You don't know."

Mr. Badger came to the archway. "There you are. Still eating? I hope we're not rushing you, but the plane is ready to go."

"It was lovely," I said with automatic politeness, and my Greek temper began to die down as quickly as it had flared up, leaving a dry feeling like ashes, burning eyes and a hurting throat, as if scorched by smoke.

"Yes. Thank you. Will you excuse me, Athena, Bart? I need to get my things together." Montero moved away toward the atrium, and I felt as if a piece of my heart tore off and went with him, like a rag of clothing snagged on barbed wire.

"Eleutheria has put your suitcase in the car," Mr. Badger said to me.

"Then I'll be right there."

We were a quiet group in the dark car driving to the airport outside the village. Mr. Badger sat in front with the chauffeur, and I was wedged between Mr. O'Neill, returned to his workaday pinstripes, and Montero; but there was no hand holding, no surreptitious hug. We seemed separated by a wall of cold, hard misery.

Mr. Badger's plane had a sitting room with comfortable swivel chairs, each equipped with a seat belt. A narrow passage led past the galley to several cabins, each containing its own bed, a table and chair, a little closet and an airplane lavatory. My compartment was beautifully appointed, with linen sheets on the turned-back bed and Florentine paper on the leather-topped writing table. The chair, bolted to the floor and equipped with a seat belt, was upholstered in leather the color of rose brick, and there was an antique Shiraz rug on the floor.

Back in the lighted cabin, Montero seemed entirely his old self, genial, charming, ready with courteous banter, as easy with me as with the two men. It was a struggle for me to maintain an equal composure, but we conversed as two polite strangers trapped together in the body of this modern whale. Soon we taxied out onto the runway. The engines roared, the stars sped past the windows, the cabin tilted up with a clunk of landing gear, and we were airborne, bound for Brightwater.

The steward rolled in a cart holding a silver service and coffee cups, bottles of brandies and liqueurs and a platter of small sweets, petit fours and bonbons from Paris. Mr. Badger asked me to pour the coffee, and I was surprised to notice that my hands were steady. I was beyond anger now, calm in the emotionless reality of despair.

Aware that I was in for a restless night, I avoided the coffee and nursed a medicinal brandy and soda until Mr. O'Neill consulted his watch. "Indeed," he said, "the older I grow the less able I am to change time zones. So I think I will bow to necessity and say good night." He shook hands with Mr. Badger and Montero. I stood up and kissed his cheek, and he embraced me with unusual warmth and then said "Urn, hum, m'yes," and blew his nose before retiring.

"I think I'll follow suit," I said, extending a hand to Mr. Badger and then Montero, who bent and kissed my forehead, still the old family friend. It seemed like a farewell.

In my cabin, I raised the shade on the little window and looked out at the night sky. I saw the full moon and the drawn sword of Orion and the little cluster of the Pleiades, and I leaned my head against the vibrating glass. I thought of that most moving of cries from the lonely heart, the poem of *Sappho* as translated by Housman.

The rainy Pleiades wester
Orion plunges prone,
And midnight strikes and hastens,
And I lie down alone.
The rainy Pleiades wester
And seek beyond the sea
The head that I will dream of
That will not dream of me.

He was not beyond the sea, only on the other side of the bulkhead. But all the oceans of the world could not have separated us more completely.

The great hollow cave of my empty heart had spread its chill so that I shivered. "I wanted you to be free," my father had said. His wish had come true. I was a stranger, an outsider, but I was free.

Forever.

CHAPTER TWENTY

There was no question of sleep, even in that interminable transatlantic night, and I had brought nothing to read. After pacing the confines of my cabin, I let my eyes rest on the pretty writing table with its box of Florentine paper and the tooled leather stand holding two expensive pens. The plane gave a shudder and a sudden drop. I sat down at the table, fastened my seat belt, and picked up the pen. It was there, above the Alps on the unhappiest night of my life, that I began to write this account.

I lost track of both time and place, so it was with a momentary sense of bewilderment that I heard movements in the hall outside my cabin. It was still dark, and I was stiff and sore from sitting still for so long. I washed and changed from that ill-fated dinner dress. I put on my last clean blouse and clasped around my neck the gold locket with my parents' pictures, for luck. I wore pantyhose and pumps beneath my travel-weary suit.

Ned O'Neill was in the sitting room, and the steward had unfolded a table between two chairs and was serving coffee and orange juice and a sturdy American breakfast of bacon and eggs.

"Good morning, Ned. Don't stand." I slipped quickly into the chair opposite him. "My, that looks good. May I join you?"

"Please."

The steward brought orange juice embedded in crushed ice and a fresh silver pot of coffee. I had barely quenched my thirst before he was back with a hot plate from which he whipped off a silver cover revealing a breakfast to match that of my companion.

We were mostly silent as we ate and shared the international newspaper of the previous day, but when our plates had been taken, we both leaned back and I poured us more coffee.

"Ned," I began, "I wanted to talk to you about business." He drew his little black book from his breast pocket. "And I'd like your advice as well as your help."

"As your attorney or your friend, Athena?"

"Both, I hope. You see ... well, it's about all that money." He looked mildly alarmed. "Don't worry. I'm not going to give it all away. But I would like to put part of it — maybe twenty percent... "

"Something more than a million dollars, depending on the interest accrued," Ned said, making notes.

"And set up a trust for the restoration of the Fender Manor outside of Brightwater. It is a magnificent eighteenth century house of real historical and architectural importance, but it's in a terrible state of disrepair."

He gave me an alert, questioning look. I was thankful that he could have no idea of how bad that state really was. "That could be managed, I suppose. In fact, there could be a tax advantage. Had you thought of supervising this restoration yourself? I'm afraid I have no expertise ..."

"No. The house belongs to the estate of Jared fender."

His eye widened behind their lenses.

"It's a long story, but it is entailed to Victor Courtney, a very able young man of about twenty. But there's no way he could have the means to restore or even repair it enough to make it inhabitable."

"So you wish to provide those means."

"Yes."

"It's not an unreasonable investment. Actually, quite imaginative. But you're not doing this, I hope, out of any sense of — because of the recent tragedy."

"Yes. Partly. Not because I think I caused Jared's death. I didn't. But because I would like to help his family's house to — so to speak — put its past behind it."

"I think it can be arranged. I will begin to draw up the papers as soon as I get back to my office. Do you wish the income to go to the restoration of the, ah, historic house and the capital to remain in your name?"

"My original idea was to settle the whole trust on Victor Courtney."

"And who, pray, is Victor Courtney?"

Montero's resonant voice broke into our colloquy. "He is my son," he said.

"Ah, Monty. Do join us." Ned swiveled a chair so that it faced the third side of our table. Montero was pale, and his eyes were great hollows. "Your son," Ned said making notes. "And the heir to the Fender Manor?"

The steward brought Montero's breakfast, which he began to eat, rapidly and distractedly. "He is the natural son of Jared and Emma Fender, who put him up for adoption in his infancy." He said at length. "I adopted him."

"Fender by birth, Courtney by agnation." Ned was matter-of-fact as he made more notes. "I see."

"It's much more complicated than that, Ned," Montero said. "I'm afraid that before you or I can give Athena any useful advice, you should visit the Fender manor and see the situation. It is presently in the hands of a cousin of Jared, an extremely shady character, and his son, an imbecile savant."

I had forgotten about Jasper and Jim.

Ned, however, retained his calm manner. "Athena is free to invest her fortune as she wishes."

The plane had begun its descent. Mr. Badger emerged from the captain's cabin forward of the sitting room and, after greeting us all, strapped himself into his armchair. The steward took away the breakfast trays. We were silent as the plane bumped to a landing, reversed its engines so hard that the fuselage shuddered and we were pinned to our seats like astronauts. It came to an abrupt stop, for the Brightwater airpark is very small. In European fashion, we applauded the pilot and began to breathe again.

We bade farewell to the captain and Mr. Badger and Mr. O'Neill, who were continuing on to Detroit, and descended the rolling staircase. After the stale air of even this luxurious airplane, the salt breeze of Brightwater was fresher than I remembered.

The same moon that had risen over us in Greece was setting in Brightwater as we cleared customs and handed our bags into the back of the taxi. Montero's strong profile was etched against the flame red sky as we turned off the main road and down the lane which led between stone walls toward the sea. The dawn breeze, barely stirring, brought the scent of bayberry on the salt air. From the cove we could hear the bell buoy, and in the distance the lament of the Squanocket Point Light. The sun rose, pouring horizontal shafts of gold through the dispersing fog beneath the bare trees of the apple orchard. We drove through the open gate in the wall and down the curving drive between maple trees to the front door of the big white house.

"Oh, God," said Montero, for William was standing, leaning on his cane, beneath the carved lintel of the doorway. It was the first time we had spoken alone since the previous night. His hand lay on the seat between us. I longed to take it, but I was paralyzed by my old sense of isolation. The moment passed, and he paid the driver and then held the door for me.

"Welcome home," said William, and suddenly I found that tears were streaming hopelessly down my face. He limped forward and looked at me searchingly and then turned to Montero. "Jared?" he asked.

"I'm sorry," Montero said.

"He was killed in an accident in Agios Titos," I said, still unable to stop crying. William put out his arms as if I were the one bereaved, and we clung to each other, our tears mingling, until William released me and, drawing out his handkerchief, wiped first my face and then his.

"There," he said. "There. Thank you, my dear. Now I must go and tell Veronica."

"No. I can't let you. I will." Montero had been standing aside, very much alone, and now he moved swiftly toward the jeep, which he mounted, kicked into action, and drove away up the drive.

William watched him until he had left the gate and disappeared up the lane. Then, taking my hand, he moved toward his own car, an aged Volvo fitted with a hand throttle, for it was his right foot that was damaged.

"Dear Monty," he said as he opened my door. He slid in beside me and started the engine. "Just like his father, my brother Luke. He has to manage everything and everybody. Well, poor lad. God knows we have let him do it all these years, to our benefit."

"I think he feels especially responsible," I said, "because he was there. He tried to save Jared. He nearly went over the cliff himself."

"Poor Jared. He was a time bomb. He carried the seeds of his own destruction." My tears had started again and I wondered if they would ever stop. I realized in that aching hollow of my heart that I wept less for Jared than for Monty and me and our own inexorable fate.

William took his hand off the throttle briefly, causing us to slow down so suddenly that the truck behind us blared its horn and changed lanes. He gripped my hand and then resumed his former speed. "Homer knew everything," he said at length, staring straight ahead at the windshield. "'The women wept, each remembering her own sorrow.'"

By the time we reached the Fenderbog Road, I had managed to dry my eyes. "I'll get the gate," I said and got out, swinging open the rusty portals on their oiled hinges. This time I left them open.

William gave me a questioning look as I resumed my seat but said nothing as we bounced over the weeds and bumps of the drive. The door of the manor stood open, and we stepped into the hall. We heard low voices from the drawing room at our right. A streamer of dust crawled over the toe of my shoe. William straightened his shoulders and stepped into the drawing room. I followed him.

Montero stood with his back to us, and Mrs. Fender, her hand resting on a wing chair of tattered damask, faced him, her head thrown back, so that, with her dark, aquiline beauty, she looked almost regal. Then she saw William and walked into his arms.

He bent his head over hers, and I realized that the two beautiful old people were kissing. Really kissing. Montero and I backed out of the room and shut the door very quietly.

At the side of the jeep he stopped. He looked dazed. "We have to talk," he said. "Veronica asked me to tell you something ... I can't quite understand it ..."

"Let's go back to the Castle. I'll make us some coffee. Nobody in Greece knows how to make good coffee."

My room at the Castle was filled with the morning sun, made more radiant by the reflection from the sea, which cast ripples of light across the ceiling. In this brightness, Montero's face looked gaunt and sad as I brought our two cups to a little table by the window seat. "Veronica said the most extraordinary thing," he said. "She sent you a message, 'Tell Athena that they are both free and happy.' I don't know who she meant. And she said that she heard the shot and found Silas and that he died in her arms."

"Madame Ursula and Silas. They saved my life at the manor."

"Veronica said the same thing. It ... it hardly seems believable."

"That's why I want to help Victor bring it back."

"I would have been happy to let that place rot away into the bog. How strange it seems that you understand the Manor in a way I never did." He turned away, looking out at the water. "I should have listened to you," he said.

"You wanted the best for me. You couldn't know."

"But I could have listened." He still looked out to sea. His profile looked to me as remote as the rocky headlands behind him. I could hardly breathe. At length he spoke again. "I suppose I have lost the right to ask you to stay."

"No," I said. He turned quickly to face me. "Even if you don't ... even if it's all off between us, I'll stay here, as your friend, your assistant, if you'll have me."

He turned that dark blue gaze full on me. "I'll need time to learn to trust people to manage for themselves. You'll have to teach me."

"I'm only learning myself. I'm sorry I got so mad, Monty. My father was always so dominating. And I loved him so much. And, with all that's been going on, I really haven't had time to grieve properly. Oh, shoot, I'm crying again."

He cradled my head in his hands, threading his fingers through my hair. "But his heart died long ago, with Sophie. We Courtney's have hearts that never give out. And you have mine. Forever. Nothing will change that."

I tilted up my face to meet his lips in a long, hungry kiss. At length he raised his head, his eyes full of wonder, and started to speak, but I said, "Shush." He kissed me again, pulling me close, his hand stroking my back and hip and thigh and then slipping under my knees until he lifted me up and carried me to the bedroom and lay down beside me. His hands were very gentle at first until, pulling away with reluctance, I got myself free of my clothes and helped him with his buttons and zippers. My skin felt like silk against the long hard planes of his body as we were transported beyond all sorrow, all fear, all thought until it seemed as if all of his being were drawn into mine and soon we rested together, warm and close, an occasional shudder, like an earthquake aftershock, running through us both. I stroked the thick waves of his hair. "This is better than last night," I murmured.

"That was dreadful. You don't know how I wanted to go and break down your door."

"You should have. That would have startled Ned O'Neill." We laughed gently and soon slept, making up for the deprivations of the night. When we woke several hours later it was to a new happiness, and we lost all sense of time exploring each other and the wonder of this complete abandonment to our love. We talked sometimes, whispering like two conspirators among the rumpled sheets until our desire would mount again and sweep us both away. We slept again and awoke in the afternoon, perfectly rested and ravenously hungry.

"I suppose we should go out to Bluecove," I said later, emerging from the shower, wrapped in a towel. He was in trousers and shirt on the windowseat, tying his shoes, and he looked up and held out his arms. "Are you as happy as I am?" he asked.

"Yes," I said.

Monty held my hand as we walked up the flagstone path to the door of the house at Bluecove, and when Maude opened it, she gave us a searching look and then embraced us both before either of us could speak. "Welcome home," she said. "This will be a celebration indeed."

Out of the shadows behind her stepped old William Courtney, and, on his arm, slim and straight, his Veronica.

Victor, handing around champagne in the drawing room, was dressed up for the occasion, wearing a grey flannel suit borrowed from Monty and his own Birkenstocks. "I wanted you for a stepmother the first time I saw you," he said with a grin. Monty cleared his throat uneasily. We had both been worried about how to break the news of his inheritance.

"Victor, Jared Fender left a will ..." Victor, arrested in the act of filling my glass, stood still and alert. "He names you as his heir to both the gallery in New York and the Manor."

"Awesome!" His brown eyes were alight. He closed his fist and punched the air with the gesture of a successful athlete. "Yes! It's the most beautiful house on the Point. It's like a dream. I've always had this fantasy of living there, bringing it back to what it was." He stopped and looked straight at Monty. "The thing of it is Dad, that I've known that Jared was my birth father since I was about six. Jim Fender told me when we were both in first grade at the Quaker school. He was about twelve then. I didn't understand the specifics, but, then, there's a lot you don't understand when you're six. Then I heard, from others ... like Gus. You know there aren't any secrets in Brightwater, Dad."

"But you never mentioned it," Monty said, bewildered.

"I tried often enough," Victor grinned. "But it always sent the family into such an uproar. Remember when I asked why you looked like Jared?"

"That was a memorable scene," Maude said, and the family laughed.

"But it didn't matter to me at all, you know," Victor finished, his heart in his eyes. "You were my only father. I was pretty lucky." Monty's eyes filled. William blew his nose. Recovering himself, Monty cleared his throat and spoke briskly.

"The Manor's a godawful mess, son. There's supposed to be a ghost ..."

"I think she's at rest now," I said, and Veronica's bright glance met mine.

"She is," she said. It was the first time I had heard her speak, and her voice was low and melodious. She has the gift, I thought. She, too, reads minds.

"And then there are the relatives," Monty pursued.

"Jasper and Jim went to California, after Silas died," Veronica said. "Jared had settled a little capital on them. They are in the process of buying a gas station in Marin County. I think they will do very well."

"I know it will be hard, fixing up the property, and it'll take time ..." Victor began, but I interrupted him.

"Well, there's been some money invested in a trust, to help you with the restoration," I said, and I felt my color rising.

"Awesome!" Victor repeated. He looked around at the faces of his family in wonder. "You know, I have to declare a major this spring, and I've wanted to go into architecture and design. But I knew you wanted another archeologist in the family, Dad, so I would have done that. But now you have Athena." And he hugged me and his father and there was general laughter and we all drank a toast to all of us.

∗∗∗∗

Three weeks later we were married in the garden at Bluecove, with only the family and Gus Howe, Mr. O'Neill, and Miss Adams, fully recovered and chipper in her retirement, in attendance. I finally met Monty's tall quiet sister Margaret and her son Willy Robinson. There was a superficial resemblance between us in the fair skin and mop of dark curls, but Willy was already several inches taller than I.

The dinner after the ceremony was lively, with the conversation running an emotional course from the news of Emma's trial, exoneration and disappearance and that of William and Veronica's plans for a quiet wedding in a few months. They had decided to move into the small farmhouse on the Manor property. Victor and the Fenderbog Trust were already hard at work restoring it. Maude had taken rooms at Captain Tinwhistle's Villa, the apartment house favored by Old Brightwater, while she looked for a house in the city close to the theater. It was rumored that she had a new beau, but none of us had met him.

It was after midnight before the family dispersed and Monty and I lay together in the ancestral four poster. The breeze from the sea stirred the white curtains and brought again the sound of the bell buoy and the distant foghorns.

"What was it" he asked, raising his head from where it had lain, "that Will said that time about Robert, the first time you came to Bluecove? A poem. It made you cry. I wanted to carry you off then and there, but I couldn't get you away from Maudie."

"He was quoting a Shakespeare sonnet," I said sleepily, drawing his head back down.

But if the while I think on thee, dear friend,
All losses are restored, and sorrows end.

Ellen Brady Finn

Ellen Brady Finn grew up on the sea coast of New England and studied Classical Archeology in college. A retired high school teacher and the mother of five children and grandmother of six, she now lives in a village outside of Detroit.

Made in the USA
Charleston, SC
08 June 2015